More RETURN TO FEAR STREET

You May Now Kill the Bride

RETURN TO FEAR STREET

THE
WRONG
GIRL

R.L. STINE

HARPER TEEN
An Imprint of HarperCollinsPublishers

HarperTeen is an imprint of HarperCollins Publishers.

The Wrong Girl

Library of Congress Control Number: 2018945992
ISBN 978-0-06-269427-0

Typography by Jenna Stempel-Lobell
 21 22 PC/LSCH 10 9 8 7 6 5 4 3
❖
First Edition

THE
WRONG
GIRL

My name is Poppy Miller, and I am not a criminal.

Yes, robbing the store seemed like a great idea. It was all supposed to be for fun. My friends and I were bored, and we wanted to be famous. We wanted everyone to think we were brave and outrageous.

And I have to admit I was trying to impress Jack Sabers. Show him how bold I could be, how daring. Sure, I was crushing on Jack, but there was something else. I guess deep down, I wanted to be as *dangerous* as Jack.

I didn't really think about it at the time. The robbery idea just came from out of nowhere. And the next thing I knew, my friends and I were pulling black ski masks over our heads and preparing to burst into Harlow's Pic 'n' Pay and perform our stickup.

Yes, it was all in fun. Fun. Remember that. Manny had his phone raised, ready to video the whole thing, ready to put our bold robbery online for everyone to enjoy.

But things don't always go the way you planned—*do* they?

My heart was pumping—not with fear but with excitement. My skin actually tingled. I'd never felt so alert, aware of every sound, every flash of color.

It was all happening in slow motion . . . Ivy tucking her hair carefully under the mask . . . Jeremy smoothing down the front of his T-shirt as if he wanted to look good on the video . . . Manny's dark eyes sparkling through the mask eyeholes.

We pushed up to the glass front door. Stepped into the bright light from the store. As if stepping into a spotlight onstage. So totally exciting.

But when Jack slipped the pistol into my hand . . . pushed the little gun into my palm and closed my hand around it . . . everything changed.

We'd never talked about using a gun. It wasn't part of the plan.

I didn't want it. I wanted to drop it. I wanted to let go.

But my fingers wouldn't move. It was as if they were locked.

It weighed a ton in my hand. It was *burning* my hand. But I couldn't let go.

And when Mr. Harlow, the store owner, reached into his cash drawer behind the counter, his eyes wide with surprise and anger . . . when he reached into the drawer, *the gun went off.*

The gun in my hand went off—and my life was changed forever.

PART ONE

SIX WEEKS BEFORE THE ROBBERY

PART ONE

1

POPPY NARRATES

Ever feel like you're a dry brown leaf in a big clump of dry brown leaves being swept this way then that way by swirling winds? Probably not. But I like to write poetry, and sometimes I just let my mind fly free.

You have to let your mind fly free when you're bored and restless and it's spring and you live in a nowhere town like Shadyside. You still have weeks to go in eleventh grade, and then there's the long summer to get through—maybe a boring summer job—and then a long senior year. How else are you going to spend all that time and eke out some fun and stay out of trouble?

Before Jack Sabers showed up and all the horror began, my amigos and I were bored with a capital B-O-R-E-D. Just leaves blowing aimlessly in the wind.

I mean, can you imagine—we were still hanging at the Division Street Mall. No one hangs at the mall anymore. So many stores are boarded up and the place looks like the whole country is going out of business, and even the Cinnabon has a sign on it that says it's closing at the end of May.

How can that be? Everyone loves Cinnabon.

The Burger Pit is still here, but it's expensive, and the two-dollar double cheeseburgers at Lefty's across from the high school are much better. And how boring am I, standing here talking about hamburgers with my friends? There has to be more to life, don't you think?

My name is Poppy Miller. I'm the short one with the springy straw-blond hair that looks like it's about to bounce right off my head. Yes, I have pale-blue eyes and freckles and my two front teeth stick out a little, but some people tell me that's sexy.

Do I like to have fun? Three guesses. I admit I'm always the most enthusiastic one in my crowd. But I'm serious about things, too. I'm serious about my poetry. And I'm serious about learning to become an actor. That's why I'm in the Shadyside High Drama Club.

I'm hoping to get a scholarship to the drama department at Carnegie Mellon. I know it's a long shot, but you have to give yourself challenges, right? Of course, when

Jack Sabers showed up, I took up some *wrong* challenges. But . . . don't let me get ahead of myself.

The tall, skinny guy with the short brown hair and the serious expression is my boyfriend, Keith Carter. I guess I have to call him my boyfriend, but I'm not really that into Keith. He's like an in-between boyfriend, if that makes any sense. It's like looking for Swiss cheese but there's none around and you have to settle for American.

Actually, Keith is more like Velveeta. Not even actual cheese. I guess his best quality is that he likes me.

Ivy Tanner is my BFF. She's the one with the broad, pale forehead, the green cat eyes, and the awesome copper-colored hair that flows in waves down past her shoulders. Ivy loves her hair. She can seldom keep her hands out of it, and I don't blame her. It shines and shimmers like ocean waves, like in the L'Oreal shampoo commercials. Seriously. Ivy has TV-commercial hair.

She's nice, too.

Ivy has been going with Jeremy Klavan since ninth grade when he moved here. He's a good guy, a little intense sometimes, spends a lot of time texting kids at his old school in Shaker Heights. Jeremy is quiet and, I guess, a little shy.

I think part of his problem is his allergies. He's, like, allergic to everything, and it makes him timid. I mean, he always has to know what's in something before he'll eat it.

He carries an inhaler and a container of pills. But when he's not sneezing or wheezing and his skin isn't breaking out in blotches, he can be fun in a quiet sort of way. He has a dry sense of humor.

Most of Jeremy's jokes go right over the head of the last member of our group, Manny Kline. Manny is big and wide and loud and a grinning fool and is always punching people and pretending to want to box with them. He doesn't have a mean bone in his body. He's just fun all the time and has a great toothy smile and makes us all laugh.

Manny is a musical genius. He can pick up any instrument and play it. But he's a wizard on guitar and on keyboard. And I should mention saxophone. He was in a band with some guys from Martinsville High, but they weren't good enough, and he got discouraged and quit.

The five of us are pretty tight. I don't know how you'd describe us. We're not in the cool clique at school. We don't live in North Hills and we don't take tennis lessons and horseback riding on Saturdays. We're not Brainiacs, although we're smart enough and we know enough to get by. We're definitely not jocks. We're the Undescribables, I think.

Ha. That's a good title for a poem.

We're just there, you know? We're just people. I mean, we all want to get somewhere or be something eventually. But it's also hard to stay motivated when spring comes and the warm air lulls you into laziness, and the air smells so sweet, it, like, teases you, and you feel so restless. It's almost an itch, I think. An uncomfortable feeling on your skin and inside you that you should have more going on.

Or is that just more poetry from Poppy Miller?

Anyway, that day we'd been wandering around the mall, and we ran into a few kids from school. No one we were really friends with.

Ivy and I looked at some sleeveless T's at TJ Maxx while the guys hung by the door, looking unhappy. I saw a scoop-neck tank top for only twenty dollars I wanted to try on, but they were looking so impatient, I said, "Skip it."

Manny had to stop and stare into the display window at Guitar World. The instruments in that window always make him drool. "I'm saving my money for that Gibson over there," he said, pointing, nose pressed against the glass. "I can feel it in my hands. It's like a baby, you know?"

"Don't get weird," Jeremy said, giving Manny a shove.

Manny laughed. "Just trying to freak you out."

"*Looking* at you freaks me out," Jeremy replied.

"It's getting late," Keith said. "I think the mall closes at nine." Keith always knows what time it is. He's the time cop in the group. He's never late for anything, which is totally weird, right? He's the only person I know who always worries about the time.

We ended up at the end of the mall. I could see the parking lot through the wide exit door. We were standing in front of the last store, Pet Haven. And two adorable white puppies pawed the window glass to get our attention.

"Awww, what are they?" Ivy asked. "Oh. The sign says shih tzu."

Manny laughed. "That's a nasty word. Who would call a dog that?"

Ivy slapped his wrist. "It's two words, and it's Chinese."

Manny gazed at the puppies behind the glass. "Do you think they speak Chinese?"

"Ohmigod, they are adorable. I want them both!" I said. "Look. That one is jumping up and down. He likes me."

"Your mom would kill you if you brought home a dog," Keith said, shaking his head. Why does he always have to be sensible? He's so totally predictable.

I ignored him. "Let's go in. I have to cuddle that dog. I mean, really."

Jeremy took a step back. "I can't go in the store," he said. "I'm allergic to dog dander."

Manny laughed. "Dog dander? Is that a thing?"

"Dog fur," Jeremy said. "I'm totally allergic."

I started to pull off the silk scarf I had around my neck. "Wrap this around your face," I said, "and maybe you'll be okay."

"No way." Jeremy backed away, motioning with both hands. "I can't wear it unless you wash it first. My skin is very sensitive and—"

"You should live in a plastic bubble," Manny said. "People would feed you through a tube in the side."

Jeremy scowled at him. "Funny," he muttered. "Do you think I like being a freak of nature? Allergic to everything?"

Manny actually blushed. "Hey, I'm sorry, man," he

said. "I didn't mean it. You're right. That was stupid. I shouldn't make fun—just because you're a freak of nature." He hee-hawed and slapped Jeremy on the back.

"Poppy thinks a scarf can solve any problem," Ivy said, trying to change the subject, I guess.

My friends are always making fun of me about the scarves I wear. But I love them. I always like to have a really colorful one draped around me.

It's not so weird. My parents took me to Paris when I was ten, and all the women wore beautiful, stylish scarves over there. So I adopted the habit. It's kind of like my trademark.

Ivy pointed to the store window. "That puppy has his eyes on you, Poppy. Look at his little tail snapping back and forth. Ha. That's hilarious. Like a cartoon."

I started to pull open the glass front door. And if I had continued walking into the store without glancing to one side, everything would have been fine, and maybe none of the nightmare things would have happened.

But I stopped and glanced at the doors from the parking lot, which slid open, and I stared at the boy who strode into the mall. I recognized him. Jack Sabers. I didn't know him. But I'd seen him around school, and people talked about him a lot. The word they usually used when they talked about Jack was "trouble."

He looks tough. He has a sharp jaw that looks like it could cut you. And strange silvery eyes—robot eyes, that you can't read. He's normal height, but he walks with a strutting step, like a cowboy or something, that makes him look taller. His hair is white-blond and spiky. No one else at Shadyside High has that kind of punk hair. Not anymore.

Jack hasn't been at our school for long. I don't know where he came from. I mean, until that night, we'd never spoken a word to each other. But I'd noticed him a lot. And a few times, I thought I'd caught him looking at me.

And he was looking at me now, one hand on the pet-store door, the puppies yapping through the window glass. Jack had this stern expression on his pale face as his gaze moved slowly from one of us to another. He nodded to himself. I guess our faces clicked in and he recognized us from school.

I watched him strut toward us, such a peculiar bob-bing walk, as if he was moving to a silent beat. His faded denims were shredded at both knees. He wore a gray sleeveless T-shirt with the letters *UFO* in blue across the chest. As he came closer, I saw the gold stud in one ear and a small tattoo of a blackbird on the back of his right hand.

He slid his hands into his jeans pockets. "What's up?"

"The moon," Manny said, pointing up.

Jack sneered. "I've seen you at school. You're the funny guy, right?"

Manny grinned. "Sometimes."

"We're just hanging," I said. I couldn't believe his eyes. They were like silvery mirrors.

He studied me for a long moment. "You bored?"

Ivy and I nodded. Keith took a step back. Maybe Jack made him nervous.

"Not much happening here," Jeremy said.

A tight-lipped grin spread over Jack's face. He leaned toward me, until he was almost touching me. "Want to do something dangerous?"

2

POPPY CONTINUES

I caught a flash of fear in Keith's eyes. We were all staring hard at Jack now. He certainly got our attention.

"What do you mean, dangerous?" Keith asked. He put one hand on my shoulder.

Jack's grin faded. He scratched the side of his face. "Not really dangerous. Just a prank. You know. A joke."

I suddenly realized my heart had started to beat a little faster. Ivy shifted her long hair off her face. "You want to play a joke? On who?" she asked.

Jack pointed into the pet-store window. The two puppies had given up and were lying side by side in their crate. "McNulty," Jack said. "He owns this store."

I squinted into the store. "The bald guy in there?"

Jack nodded. "He fired me today for no reason."

"You were working here?" Manny asked.

"Yeah. Just cleaning up and stuff. Stacking the dog food. You know. Just being a slave."

"Why did he fire you?" Keith asked.

Jack shrugged. "I told you. No reason." He took a few steps back so McNulty couldn't see him through the window. "You guys are bored, right? So you want to help me with my little joke?"

Keith waved a hand. "I don't think so."

"Don't listen to Keith. Tell us your joke," I said.

Jack rubbed his cheek. "Well . . . I've got fifteen stray dogs headed to the kennel in my truck. I thought maybe it might be kind of awesome to let them all loose in McNulty's store."

Manny and Jeremy laughed. "Awesome."

"No way," Keith insisted. So typical of him to back away from a little fun.

What did I see in him?

"That could be a riot," Ivy said, brushing her hair back again.

"Count me out," Keith said. He turned and started to walk away.

"Hey, it's totally harmless," I called after him. "It's not a crime or anything. It's just a joke."

Manny raised his phone. "I saw a YouTube video. Some guys did this in Chicago. It went viral. They're, like, famous. I've got to video this. It's crazy. Crazy."

A thin smile crossed Jack's face. "Cool. We can be famous, too. "I'll back my truck up to the door. Then you'll help me herd the dogs into the store."

"Sweet," I said. My skin was tingly. I guess I was a little excited. And I felt myself drawn to Jack. Pulled to him, almost against my will, as if he were a powerful magnet.

I knew he was trouble. Everyone knew he was trouble. But we were bored and we were restless, so we went along with his prank.

And, of course, that was the start of more trouble than I could handle.

3

POPPY CONTINUES

The dogs came out of the back of Jack's pickup squealing and barking and yapping their heads off. I don't know who was more excited—us or them.

Luckily, it was near closing time. So there was no one in this back hall to try to stop us. We couldn't really stop the dogs anyway. They followed each other, tails waving furiously, into the mall, toenails clicking on the marble floor, directly into the pet store.

Jeremy held the store door open. We barely had to herd them. They seemed to know exactly where they were supposed to go. They were mostly a shaggy mess. Some big dogs, shepherd mixes or something, I don't really know dogs. One huge black one with clumps of fur almost down to the floor, was the size of a small horse. There were small ones, too, squeaking and clucking, scraggly creatures, not cute.

I heard screams from inside the store. I guess Mr. McNulty was catching on to what was happening. Manny couldn't stop laughing. He had his phone held high and was recording the stampede of dogs. I heard howls and a crash, and McNulty was cursing his head off now.

Ivy and I followed the last dog into the store in time to see the big black dog rise up and knock McNulty over. I heard glass shatter. It was a long, narrow store. Jack's dogs were squeezed in the aisle. And then it got noisier as some of the pet-store dogs broke out and came running to join the party, and their barks and howls of joy drowned out McNulty's curses.

"Check that out!" Manny bumped my shoulder from behind and pointed. A large gray mutt had managed to chew open a big bag of dog food, and the dogs were going nuts—they must have been hungry—clawing and pouncing on each other, yapping and squealing, desperate to join in the dinner party as the meaty brown bits tumbled from the bag.

McNulty was lost behind a mountain of dogs. A tall

wooden stool had been knocked over and lay on its side in the aisle. Dogs had climbed onto the front counter. More pet-store dogs came running from a back room. I have no idea how they escaped. Had the newcomers set them free?

I heard another crash as dogs knocked over a tall pile of plastic food dishes. Dogs were fighting now, snarling and snapping at each other to get to the open food bag.

The sound was deafening, but I could still hear the store owner cursing and screaming. "I'm calling 911! I'm calling 911! I'm calling the police!"

I couldn't stop laughing. It was just so insane! Like one of those ancient silent comedies my dad had showed me when I was little.

Manny was laughing, too. Jeremy had his hands over his ears. Maybe he's allergic to loud noises, too. Ivy had picked up one of the white puppies from the front window and was cuddling it against her.

Manny stopped recording and lowered his phone. He turned to Jack, who had a broad smile frozen on his face. "Are we done here?"

"Yep," Jack said. "Come on. Let's get out of here."

"Hey—what about the dogs?" I had to shout over the squeals and barks.

"Not our problem," Jack said. He grabbed my hand and pulled me to the front door. The others scattered. Ivy and Jeremy started to jog to the other end of the mall, where Jeremy had parked. I looked for Keith. I'd actually forgotten about him. Had he just gone home and left us?

"You need a ride?" Jack asked.

And that's how I ended up in his truck. But how I ended up kissing him, wrapped in his arms . . . Well . . . I'm not sure how that happened.

He was making the truck roar, showing off its speed, making it slide, as we headed to my house up near River Ridge. I knew he was showing off for me. He didn't say much. I think he thinks that's part of what makes him so cool. He's quiet and mysterious. Those silver-gray eyes always seem to be far away, like he's thinking of important things, like he's not entirely with you.

That's what I thought, riding home with him. And when he parked at the bottom of my driveway and slid his arms around my shoulders and pulled me against him, I hesitated. "I have a boyfriend," I said, but it came out in a shaky voice I didn't recognize.

"That's cool," he whispered. Then he pressed his mouth against mine, and I didn't think about Keith for a minute.

4

POPPY CONTINUES

My sister, Heather, was waiting for me inside the house.

"Hey."

"Hey."

She followed me to my room, waving her phone in one hand.

If you saw us standing side by side, you'd never guess we were sisters, and you'd never guess we're just a year apart. Heather is one year younger. She looks like Dad, and I look like Mom.

(When our parents split up, I think Heather wanted to go live with Dad. But the court wouldn't allow it.)

I'm small and thin and, I guess, dainty, if that's still a word. I'm not sure anyone says that. As I've said, I'm fair-skinned with pale-blue eyes and lots of freckles around my nose, and I have bobbing curls of straw-blond hair. Heather is nearly six inches taller than I am. She isn't fat or anything, but . . . well . . . she's big. Strong. Could probably take on some of the Shadyside basketball team if she had to.

She has short straight black hair that she keeps buzzed on one side, and a round face with big dark eyes. She hates having to wear glasses. She says it makes her look like a giant owl. I wish she wasn't always so down on herself, because she's actually very cute. But she's the poster girl for Low Self-Esteem. Seriously.

Heather had an oversized gray sweatshirt pulled down over black tights. Her hair was brushed to one side so that it looked like she'd been out in a strong wind.

I lifted Mr. Benjamin, my pet rabbit, from his cage, carried him to my bed, and set him down in my lap. I petted the soft fur on his back, and he wiggled his ears to show he liked it.

My mom is allergic to dogs, so Mr. Benjamin was a compromise. But he's a good pet, very sweet and quiet, and petting him always calms me down.

Heather, I could see, was not calm. She stood in the middle of my room, waving her phone. "I saw it," she said. Her eyes flashed behind her glasses. I couldn't tell if she was angry or excited or what.

I squinted at her. "Saw it?"

She nodded. "The pet-store video. On Instagram. I watched the whole thing."

I waited for her to continue, but she didn't. I could still taste Jack's lips on mine, and I felt kind of jumpy. I mean, the adrenaline was rushing, and I kept thinking about how nice the whole thing was, even though it shouldn't have happened.

"It was funny, right?" I prompted her.

"You could have taken me with you," she said. She set the phone down on my dresser and crossed her arms in front of her. "I like to have fun, too, you know."

I let out an exasperated sigh. I could see this discussion was about to start up all over again. Believe me, it wasn't the first time. I could recite this conversation word for word.

"When I went to the mall, I didn't know—" I started.

She didn't let me finish. "I asked you at dinner if I could come," she said, her voice becoming tight, almost choked. "I practically begged you."

I rolled my eyes. "Heather, please. Do we have to have this discussion again? What do I always tell you?"

Behind the glasses, her dark eyes narrowed in anger. "That I have to have my own friends."

"Right," I said. "You can't—"

"But that's crap," she snapped, practically spitting the words. I saw her cheeks darkening to pink. "I'm only a year younger than you, and you treat me like I'm a baby."

"But—"

"Or you just ignore me completely."

"That's not true!" I cried, jumping to my feet. I placed Mr. Benjamin back in his cage. "I hang out with you all the time, Heather."

"Liar."

"I took you with me to see *Hamlet* at the Martinsville Town Center last week."

She uttered a bitter laugh. "Only because none of your friends wanted to go with you. You even asked Rose Groban to go with you—and you hate Rose Groban."

Her chest heaved up and down as she started to breathe hard. Her face was a dark red now, nearly purple. Heather knows how to be angry. It's kind of her hobby. Scowling, she started to pace back and forth, her sneakers thudding on the carpet.

"What exactly are you saying?" I demanded. "That every time I go somewhere with friends, I have to ask you along? Are you saying that my friends have to be your friends, too?"

"No. I—I—I—" she sputtered. "I'm just saying that I like to have fun, too. Your friends all know me. You could ask me to come with you. Sometimes you could ask me, you know?"

"But what about *your* friends?" I demanded. I knew I should shut up. I should stop this dumb shouting match. I knew I couldn't win it. So why was I keeping it going? "Your friends—"

"I don't have any friends!" Heather screamed. She grabbed a big silver trophy off my bookshelf, my Drama Club trophy from last year. I gasped as she pulled her arm back—and heaved the trophy across the room.

We both screamed as the trophy whirred past my head, smashed into the wall behind me—and stuck there. She had heaved it so hard, it stuck in the plaster!

I stood there in shock, staring at my sister, my heart doing flip-flops, my hands pressed against my cheeks. I could barely breathe.

It was the first time . . . the first time I realized that Heather could be dangerous.

5

POPPY CONTINUES

"See? We *are* going to be famous," Ivy said.

I shifted my phone to the other ear and continued brushing my hair. "Why? What are you talking about?"

"Our pet-store video. Over ten thousand views. And Manny told me BuzzFeed picked it up."

"Wow." To be honest, I wasn't thinking about becoming famous. I was thinking about Jack . . . his arms around me . . . kissing him that night.

"What should we do next?" Ivy said. "We need to start a channel."

I set the hairbrush down. "No time. I have to go. I have the play audition."

"Break a leg," Ivy said, and clicked off.

Taking a deep breath, I checked myself out in the mirror and headed downstairs.

I have a lot of confidence in myself as an actress. I know I have some good skills. Mom let me take private acting lessons at the Players Theater School in Garden Grove, even though they were expensive, and I think I learned a lot there.

But, no matter how much confidence you have, auditions always make you nervous. A few minutes later, as I made my way down the aisle to the front of the auditorium at school, my hands were icy and damp, and I definitely felt my heart jumping around in my chest like it was playing leapfrog.

(I have to remember that image for a poem.)

Mr. Gregory is the Drama Club adviser at Shadyside High. We all call him Mr. G. He wrote an original play for our annual presentation. It's a horror-thriller called *Don't Go There!* It's mainly about six teenagers trapped in an abandoned hotel, and some kind of supernatural being starts haunting them and taking them out one by one.

I was trying out for the part of Becka Hastings. Becka is the smartest girl in the group. She's kind of the leader, and she's the one who discovers the secret of the old hotel.

I liked this role because Becka is smart and funny, but

she also gets to scream a lot. I'd practiced screaming in my room for several days and, even though I had my door closed, I'd managed to drive my mom and sister nuts, and they had to beg me to shut up. When it comes to theater, I dive into the deep end. No shallow waters for me.

I'd memorized all of Becka's lines, the whole part. And I knew I could do an awesome audition for Mr. G, but, of course, there was Rose Groban, my rival, my comic-book archenemy, the evil Rose Groban, who didn't even pretend to be my friend.

Rose always acts as if she pities me. Not sure why. She gets this superior look on her face, and then everything she says is ironic and passive-aggressive and said with a kind of indulgent chuckle, like I'm a child she is forced to put up with.

Yes, there was Rose Groban. And what role would she want to pounce on? Becka Hastings, of course. So here we were, trapped in this endless competition, as we had been ever since she transferred to Shadyside in fourth grade.

As I made my way down the aisle, I counted about twenty kids ready to audition for *Don't Go There!* They filled the first three rows of the auditorium. Some were talking quietly. A few were on their phones. Others were reading scripts. Mr. G stood on the stage in front of the tall purple curtain, adjusting a floor microphone, so I guessed we would have to go up there and audition in front of all the others when our names were called.

I took a seat at the end of the fourth row, and Rose Groban appeared at my side instantly, as if by black magic. Did I mention that she is beautiful? Really. A stunner. Just gorgeous, as my mother would say. (And has said.)

She has round brown eyes and beautiful long lashes, a broad forehead, a perfect nose, high cheekbones like a fashion model, skin as smooth as milk, a smile bright enough to see in the dark, and cascades of wavy black hair, perfect hair that tumbles over her shoulders and nearly halfway down her back, somehow always in place.

She's beautiful, and now she was standing in the aisle, one hand on the back of my chair, gazing down at me. "Poppy, I saw the pet-store video," she said. "What were you thinking?"

"It . . . was a joke," I said. "You know. Supposed to be funny."

"Yes. Funny," she repeated, as if she'd never heard that word before. She tossed her hair back. "Well, all I kept thinking was, I hope Poppy takes a shower after handling all those ugly stray mutts. Who knows what kind of diseases they were carrying."

"Hey, thanks for thinking of me," I said. Sometimes I try to be as sarcastic as Rose, but I don't always pull it off.

"I'm feeling good about the audition," Rose said, even though I hadn't asked. "I did a quick script run-through at breakfast this morning. But I didn't want to over-rehearse, you know? I mean, I like to feel loose and spontaneous up there."

"Me too," I said.

Her eyes narrowed with sudden concern. "Poppy, what's your second choice? Which role do you want if you don't get Becka? I mean, I'll probably get Becka. So what other role do you think you'd like? I was thinking about it because I was concerned about you. And I think Gretchen, the weird old lady, might be an exciting challenge for you. Something you could get the most out of."

Was she kidding me? The old lady? The lamest part in the play? Gretchen doesn't even appear until the last ten minutes!

I laughed out loud.

"I was just thinking you don't want to be too disappointed," Rose said. "You should definitely have an alternate plan. You know. Just in case."

"Rose, I *know* what you were thinking," I said.

That made her blink.

Onstage, Mr. G tapped the microphone. "People, I believe we're all here. Let's get started. I'm going to audition the role of Becka Hastings first. I need you all to listen and watch carefully. Put your phones away, please. And don't be nervous, everyone. You're among friends. You can feel the support in the room, can't you?"

Not with Rose standing over me. No, I thought, *I don't feel the support, Mr. G.*

Mr. G shielded his eyes from the bright lights with one hand and surveyed the rows of kids. "Poppy?"

I jumped when I heard my name.

"Poppy? Want to audition first?"

I climbed to my feet. I felt my heart leap up into my throat. To my surprise, Rose didn't step back. She blocked my way to the aisle.

"Rose—?"

She lowered her head and brought her lips close to my ear. "One more thing," she said in a raspy whisper. "I don't mean to be unsubtle. But stay away from Jack. He's not your type."

Her words caught me by surprise. My script fell from my hands and hit the floor. I felt my throat tighten and started to choke. To hide my shock, I bent down and collected the script.

Get it together, Poppy.

I knew I was overreacting, but her warning had just been so unexpected.

Had she seen us together in his truck? Or had she only seen us together in the pet-store video?

I was still fluttery when I climbed onto the stage, and I kept clearing my throat as I stepped up to Mr. G. I tried to push Rose's words from my mind. I mean, what was the big deal, really? Why should I be so surprised that Rose would say something nasty to me?

"I'll read the part of Christopher," Mr. G said. "Let's start on page six. Where they first step into the house."

I took a deep breath and flipped through the pages of the script. *You can do this, Poppy. You've practiced enough.* A low hiccup escaped my throat.

Mr. G squinted at me. "Do you need water?"

I shook my head. "No. I'm okay." I glanced down from the stage. All eyes were on me. Rose was leaning against the auditorium wall, the only one not sitting down. I guessed she was getting ready to audition next. Or maybe she just wanted me to see her there watching me.

My stomach gurgled. I wondered if Mr. G could hear it.

He began, reading the part of Christopher: "This old house *has* to be haunted. Any house with cobwebs like this has to be haunted, right?"

"I hope you're right, Christopher," I read. "I've always wanted to see a poltergeist."

Mr. G raised his eyes from his script. "The word is pol-ter-geist, Poppy."

I blinked. "I know. What did I say?"

"You said pollergeist."

I caught the smile on Rose's face. A few kids whispered in the seats below me.

"Sorry," I said. "Do-over?"

We started again, but I didn't get much better. I knew even as I was acting up there that I was totally screwing up. And when it came time for me to shriek in horror at the end of the scene, a cough interrupted my scream.

"Thank you, Poppy," Mr. G said, waving me to the stage stairs.

The kids in the seats didn't make a sound. Sometimes they applaud when someone gives a really good audition. My hand was icy and wet on the railing as I stepped down from the stage. I curled my script into a tight roll. I wanted to pound it against the wall.

"Rose Groban?" Mr. G called from the stage. "You can be next."

I turned away from her as she approached the steps so I wouldn't have to see her smug face. And I gasped when I saw the familiar figure storming down the aisle toward me.

"Heather?" I cried. "What are you doing here? And what are you doing with that knife?"

Her eyes were wide, crazy. She didn't answer. She stopped a few feet from me. Kids turned to see what was happening. Before I could call out, before I could scream, Heather raised the knife high—and plunged it deep into her own chest.

6

POPPY CONTINUES

I heard gasps. Screams rang out.

Heather pulled the knife blade from her chest and laughed. "Did I get you? You really believed it?" She pushed the blade into the handle, then let it pop out. "It's a stage knife. Didn't you recognize it? I found it in the Drama Club prop closet downstairs."

She plunged it into her chest and pulled it out again.

Kids were shaking their heads, chattering about my sister's little joke. "Am I missing something?" Mr. G called from the stage. "Is there another show going on down there?"

"Sorry, Mr. G," I called. I grabbed Heather's arm and pulled her toward the side of the auditorium. "That was very funny. A riot," I said, rolling my eyes. Onstage, Rose had begun her audition. She said the word *poltergeist* perfectly.

"Let go of my arm." Heather tugged herself free. I hadn't realized I was gripping her so tightly.

"What are you doing here?" I asked.

"I came to audition," she said. She scowled at me, the patented Heather Miller scowl that could make milk go sour and paint curl off the wall. "You're not the only talented one in the family, you know."

I sighed. "Did you see my audition? Not too impressive talent-wise."

Onstage, Rose was finishing up. She gave a piercing horror-movie scream that actually made my skin tingle. *She wins,* I thought. Maybe Mr. G will let me do Gretchen.

"I got a script from Mr. G last week," Heather said. "I'm going to audition for Claire. It's a small part, but she's kind of funny. I think I can be funny."

I flashed her a thumbs-up. I didn't know what else to say. Heather had never shown any interest in the Drama Club before. Was she just copying me? Or was this a good thing—Heather finding something she really wanted to devote herself to?

I didn't want to be discouraging. But she had already given up on her keyboard lessons and her horse dressage and her online "Secrets of the Universe" college course, and just about everything else she had ever tried.

Kids applauded as Rose stepped down from the stage. Mr. G called Sari Bakshi to the stage. Sari was also auditioning for Becka. She was new to our school, so I didn't know how she rated as an actress. I wanted to sit down and watch her audition, but Heather grabbed my arm.

"Will you stay for my tryout?"

Her intensity startled me. She suddenly looked so needy. "Of course," I said. "I wouldn't miss it. I'll be here rooting for you."

I was trying to be nice but my words sounded phony. She noticed. Her mouth twitched into a two-second frown. "I . . . wanted to surprise you," she said.

I laughed. "Well, you certainly made an entrance." I lowered my gaze to the stage knife, still clasped in her hand.

"I've memorized all of Claire's lines," Heather said. "It wasn't so hard. You know I've always had a good memory."

She'd always had a good memory for the supposed crimes I had committed against her. I don't think she ever forgot any argument we had or any fight or disagreement about anything. Heather could bring up something that upset her when she was five just as easily as something that happened last weekend.

"I'm sure you'll be great," I said. Why did I sound so fake? Was I upset that she was invading my space? Drama Club had always been my thing.

I led Heather to a seat on the aisle in the fourth row, and we watched the other auditions. The part of Claire was the last role in the tryouts, and only one other girl besides Heather was interested in the part.

"This is a lock," Heather whispered, squeezing my hand.

Mr. G called Heather up to the stage. Her footsteps echoed loudly on the wooden stage floor because the auditorium was nearly empty. Most everyone had auditioned and left.

As Heather began, I realized I was holding my breath. Of course, I'd never seen her act or perform. I had no way of knowing that she would be so awful. I mean, her performance was so lame, so . . . dead, I was waiting for Mr. G to hold a finger under her nose to see if she was breathing.

She said every line in a low monotone. Even though

she was speaking into a microphone, I could barely hear her. She never changed her tone, and she read everything so seriously, so earnestly, she didn't seem to realize that most of the lines were supposed to be funny.

When she finished, a smile spread over her face. Mr. G smiled back at her. "Thanks for auditioning. We'll let you know, Heather." Then he called Kathy Taylor, the other girl who wanted to be Claire, to the stage. I knew that Kathy didn't really have to audition. She had the part without saying a word.

Heather still had that triumphant smile on her face as she walked up the aisle to me. It was easy to see she was happy with her performance. Her hands were balled into tight fists and she was swinging her arms as she walked.

"Well? Poppy? What do you think?" she asked me. "Was I okay?"

I hesitated. Should I start World War III and break up the family by telling her the truth? Should I lie? Would it be better for *Heather* if I told the truth?

"You were awesome," I said.

She nodded, as if agreeing with me. "Thanks. I won't be home for dinner. Brie and I are studying for our science test together."

Brie? I'd never heard that name before. A new friend, I guessed.

I watched her trot up the aisle. I suddenly felt sorry for her. I mean, I love my sister. We used to be a lot closer, but that doesn't mean I don't love her and care about her.

And I hated to see her be so totally clueless.

Keith was waiting for me in the hall as I stepped out of the auditorium. He had been typing furiously on his phone, but he slid it into his pocket when he saw me. He kissed my cheek. "How'd it go?"

I frowned. "I would describe my audition as *not great*."

He blinked. "Not great? What does that mean?"

"I sucked out loud."

He locked his eyes on mine. "You're always so hard on yourself."

Ha. I knew he was trying to say the right thing. But I also knew that he was completely wrong. I'm almost never hard on myself. I have a totally upbeat attitude. One of my best qualities is that I never get in my own way.

I'll admit I can be hard on other people. Maybe I can be too judgmental. But I have a good, balanced view of myself. I think, unlike most kids my age, I'm confident and enthusiastic, and I've found the things I like to fill my life with.

So . . . Keith saying that I'm always hard on myself just showed how he didn't know me at all. And I suddenly found myself thinking about Jack. Truth is, I kept having flashbacks about that night we were together in his truck. And I kept wondering when I would see Jack again.

"Why are you here so late?" I asked.

"Debate Club meeting," he said. "And I wanted to catch up to you, see how the tryout went." His eyes flashed. "I can't believe you didn't kill it."

"Believe it," I said. I started toward the front doors.

He followed me. "Want to hang for a bit? Get a coffee or something? A Coke?"

I didn't want to hang for a bit. In that moment, I realized that Keith was history. I just had to figure out how to break up with him.

It wasn't Jack's fault. But Jack had helped me see that I was spending too much time with the wrong guy, a guy who didn't really ring my bells or push my buttons or whatever people say when they're trying to say they're just not crazy about someone.

"I can't," I said, walking faster, hoping to get away

without too much explanation. "I promised my mom."

"Promised her what?"

But I was out the door now, into the late afternoon sunlight, gold on the lawn in front of the high school, shadows dancing across the grass as the sun filtered through the shifting trees. The air smelled fresh and sweet, and I turned and saw that Keith hadn't followed me. A wave of relief spread over me.

Weird. I had thought I really liked Keith once. But when was that? I couldn't really remember anymore.

My house is four blocks from school. I started striding along the sidewalk, my brain spinning, a mix of Keith and Jack and my lame audition and Heather, Heather plunging that knife in her chest . . . Why did she want to frighten me like that? Was she so desperate for my attention?

I waved to some guys who drove by in a blue SUV, hip-hop music blasting from the open windows. One of them was pounding the side of the car in rhythm with the thumping beats.

I crossed the street and was halfway down the block when I saw the patrol car. Black and white, the words *Shadyside Police* in stern black letters on the door. The car slowed nearly to a stop. I could see the cop behind the wheel. His face was hidden in shadow, but I could see that he was turned toward me. Watching me.

I gave him a wave, but he didn't react. Just stared out at me. I started to walk a little faster. He inched the patrol car forward, keeping it at my side.

I turned toward him again and yelled, "Hey." But he still didn't react in any way.

I realized my heart had started bumping against my chest. My muscles tightened. This was definitely creepy. I kept walking. He kept his car sliding along with me.

I stepped off the sidewalk and began to approach him. Before I could get there, he hit the gas and roared away, tires squealing against the pavement.

I stood there watching the patrol car until it sped around a corner and vanished. A chill rolled down my back. My heart was still thumping.

What was *that* about?

I had no way of knowing that I'd be seeing him again. . . . Seeing a lot of police officers. No way of knowing that the people I cared about would start dying . . . one by one.

7

IVY CHIMES IN

On Friday night, Jeremy stayed at my house for dinner, but there was a mix-up, and he was supposed to be at his cousin's with the rest of his family. I guess they kept texting him and calling his cell for an hour. But typical Jeremy. His phone was out of power and he didn't even know it.

Sometimes I think Jeremy is a Martian or from some other planet because his head isn't always on Earth. He has a spacey quality, which I have to admit I like. He's a good guy, funny and smart, but sometimes he just zones out.

His mind drifts away on its own. Sometimes when a bunch of us are together talking about something, I glance at him and I can see that he isn't hearing a word.

What is he thinking about? I always accuse him of thinking about things back on his home planet. Jeremy says he's a royal prince on his planet and he could have me beheaded for making fun of him. Then we both laugh because we have the same twisted sense of humor.

He's not just a little flaky. Jeremy has a lot of good qualities. He will sit through all the terrible reality TV shows I love to watch, even *The Bachelor*. He doesn't make fun of me—too much—for believing everything I read in the gossip magazines and talking about those celebs as if they are my closest personal friends.

And he pretends he enjoys helping me bake cookies or a cake every weekend. I love baking things. I love the whole process. And I make an awesome treat for my family every Saturday, and Jeremy pretends he enjoys helping, when I know he'd rather be watching baseball or some other sport, or hanging out with Manny Kline, playing *World of Warcraft* or *Grand Theft Auto* on Manny's enormous flat-screen TV.

Those are his good qualities. Of course, I have to put up with all his allergies. The poor dude. He's allergic to nuts and peanuts and some dairy products and some flowers. He's even allergic to flea bites—and a mosquito bite will make his whole arm swell up and make it hard for him to breathe.

Can you imagine?

What a way to go through life. If I had those allergies, I'd just crunch myself in a corner and not go anywhere and not be any fun at all. So, in a way, Jeremy is very brave, I think.

But tonight he was an idiot, forgetting about his cousin's dinner. And why did I get blamed?

I mean seriously. My parents blamed me for inviting Jeremy over. And he blamed me, too. He said I distracted him and caused him to forget where he was supposed to be. That's kind of sweet, but of course, it's ridiculous.

And then Mom served ham tonight, and Jeremy is horribly allergic to ham, so she had to make him a tuna-fish sandwich. The whole night was basically a disaster. Not to mention I was having a bad hair night. I just couldn't get it to fall properly, and I ended up tying it back with a hair band, which I don't like to do. And it felt creaky to me. Like I hadn't entirely washed the conditioner out. You know the feeling.

I hate it when my hair makes me feel uncomfortable. It's all I can think about. I know I'm weird about it. Poppy never stops being in my face about how I'm obsessed with my hair.

So I shampooed it as soon as Jeremy left. And then I was up in my room, breezing through the new Us Weekly on my iPad when I knew I should be checking the English assignment. My phone rang—my new phone—I hadn't even had time to download half my stuff. And I couldn't hide my surprise that Keith was calling because Keith never calls me.

The new phone felt heavy in my hand. I'd bought the biggest model. A mistake? "Hey," I said. "Everything okay?" I normally wouldn't ask that, but like I said, Keith never calls me.

"Yeah. Sure. How you doing?"

"Fine. Just finding ways to put off doing any homework."

He snickered. "Is Poppy there?"

"Huh? Here? No."

"Oh. I thought maybe . . ." His voice trailed off.

"No. I haven't seen her."

"I've . . . been texting her, and she hasn't answered," he said, a little breathless.

"Maybe her phone is dead," I said. "It's been going around. It happened to Jeremy tonight."

"Ivy, have you noticed? She's been acting weird."

I hesitated. Where was he going with this? I knew Poppy was thinking of breaking up with him. We'd talked about it more than once. Actually, Poppy talked

about it a lot. She was so conflicted. After our last discussion, over two-dollar double cheeseburgers at Lefty's,
I'd actually thought she wanted *me* to decide.

"Well . . . I think Poppy is a little depressed about her
audition for the play. She doesn't think she's going to get
the part she wanted."

"I waited for her after school," Keith said. "I thought
we could talk about it, or maybe I could try to cheer her
up. You know. But she seemed in a big hurry. She didn't
even want to talk to me."

"Because of the audition," I said. "And her sister.
Heather showed up. Did you know that? Heather showed
up and auditioned, too."

"I didn't know. Poppy was surprised?"

"Uh . . . yeah."

"Poppy likes her own space," Keith said. "She probably hated Heather showing up like that."

"Probably," I said. "I think Heather is okay. I mean,
she's a little whiny, you know. A little drippy. But I always
think Poppy should give her a break."

"Has Poppy said anything to you?" Keith asked.
"About me?"

"About you? Like what?" I started to feel it getting
awkward. I'm Poppy's best friend, and I'm not going to

betray any trust between us. Besides, it's not *my* job to break up with Keith for her. If she wants to dump him, she has to do it on her own.

"Has she said anything about . . . you know . . . her and me?" Of course, he felt awkward, too. "I know she was honked off at me because I didn't stay for the pet-shop prank. But I have to be careful, Ivy. Seriously. I'm on the waiting list at Tufts, and I can't do anything crazy that'll screw me up."

"Keith—"

"My dad went to Tufts, and he's already disappointed that I'm only on the waiting list. So if I got caught in a joke like that pet-store thing, and the store owner pressed charges, and it ended up on Facebook or Instagram or something . . ."

He wanted me to say it was okay that he ran off and didn't help out with our prank. I didn't care. But I knew it had really annoyed Poppy. She's always so enthusiastic about things. I think it reminded her of just how different she and Keith are.

Keith is a nice, straight-arrow kind of guy, but he's definitely lacking in fun.

"You should talk to her," I said. The phone suddenly felt heavier in my hand. I was ready to click off.

"I'm trying to," Keith said. "But do you think there's a problem?"

"You should talk to her," I repeated. Then I had a thought. "I'm going over to her house," I said. "Maybe I could tell her you're trying to reach her."

"You're going over there?"

"Yeah. I just got a new phone, and Poppy is so good with phones. I need her to help me get back some of my apps."

"Maybe I'll swing by, too," Keith said.

"No. Why not let me talk to her? I'll tell her to give you a call."

"Oh. Okay." His voice became soft. "You know, I think Poppy is awesome."

"Me too," I said. Was he going to get all gooey? I think I liked him better when he was a stiff.

A long pause. He coughed. "Okay. Well . . . see you."

He was gone. I stared at my phone screen for a long moment, enjoying the silence. Poor guy. He was going to take this hard. And I knew it was in the cards. I'd seen the gushy look on Poppy's freckled face whenever Jack was in view.

Jack was the bad boy. The troublemaker. The wild one.

How could Keith stand a chance?

I drove to Poppy's house. I really did need help with my new phone. But I stopped when I saw the pickup truck in her driveway. Jack's truck. Jack dropping in on Poppy at ten-thirty at night.

I decided to drive on.

Poppy and Jack. Was this big news? A life-changing thing?

As it turned out, it changed all our lives. And not in a good way. Not at all.

8

POPPY NARRATES

Heather and I walked to school together. It was a gray April morning, the clouds low in the sky, threatening rain. Perfect for my mood.

I guess I felt depressed because Mr. G was scheduled to announce who'd won parts in the play, and I just dreaded having to look at the smirk on Rose Groban's face when she was announced as Becka.

I knew Mr. G would find a good part for me, maybe as Becka's sister Traci, or maybe even as the crazy old lady, Gretchen. And eventually, I'd have fun being part of the production. But it would be nice to be a winner. I could put a smirk on my face as good as Rose's if I was only given the chance.

As we walked, Heather was talking about some guy in her class she had a crush on but didn't have the nerve to talk to. I should have listened. She seldom confided in me, and I think she was really making an attempt to be close. But I tuned her out and thought about Jack.

I knew things were going too fast with him. I knew he'd been in some kind of trouble at his last school, and I knew people had issues with him, the way he roared around in that dust-covered pickup truck, and the way he sort of strutted through the halls at school, as if he was above it all. The way he kept his jaw stuck out, like he was looking for trouble. Yeah, sure. He acted tough, and that wasn't exactly the way kids rolled at Shadyside High.

But that's what attracted me, I knew.

For some reason, I kept remembering Rose's warning, the words she'd whispered in my ear just before I went onstage for my audition. Why did Rose tell me to stay away from Jack? Why did she care? What did she know about him?

Or was she just being mean? Trying to throw me off balance for my audition?

If that was the case, it had definitely worked.

"I don't think you heard a word I said," Heather

snapped, shaking her head, her eyes angry behind her round glasses.

"Of course I did," I lied.

But she took off, running ahead, backpack bouncing on her shoulders, her sneakers pounding the sidewalk loudly, and I realized our walks to school often ended this way, with her angry or disappointed in me, or whatever. I watched her charge across the street like an angry bull, without even looking to see if there were any cars coming, and I made a note to myself. I really did. *Memo to self: Be nicer to Heather.*

I ran into Manny in the hall near my locker. He was bouncing a tennis ball off the metal lockers, catching it in one hand. *Ka-chang. Ka-chang.* "Kellog isn't in homeroom today," he said. "Some strange teacher is in there. Kellog is probably hungover again."

"Good morning to you, too," I said, struggling with the combination on my locker. "What makes you think Miss Kellog is a drunk?"

Manny grinned his toothy grin, all his gums showing. "What makes you think she isn't?" *Ka-chang. Ka-chang.* Having delivered his punchline, he moved on down the hall, bouncing the tennis ball off the lockers, the sound echoing down the long hall.

Before Manny was out of sight, Rose appeared beside me, and sure enough, she had that superior smirk on her face. Her hair was pulled to one side in a single braid, perfect, not a hair out of place, and she wore a green-and-yellow summery sundress with a very short skirt, a necklace of red plastic beads around her neck. She looked awesome, and of course, she knew it.

"Just wanted to share my good news with you," she said.

I had stooped to pick up a notebook from the floor of my locker. I had the sudden urge to dive headfirst into the locker and hide in there until she left. "Good news?" I straightened up to face her. She uses some kind of citrus-type cologne so she always smells lemony.

"A scholarship." Her smile grew wider. "I got a drama scholarship for the summer at Wellesley. Do you believe it?"

She was probably expecting me to be sarcastic or to sigh in disappointment that I hadn't won it, so I decided to gush. "Oh, wow, Rose! That's awesome!" I high-fived her. Yes, I actually touched her. It was the most enthusiasm I could muster, and I think it caught her by surprise.

"Yeah, uh, I'm pumped," she said. "Now I have to find a place to live up there. Maybe an apartment of my own."

"Sweet," I murmured.

Her grin faded. It was like her lips collapsed. No, not just her lips—her whole face. She placed a hand on my shoulder. "I am so, so sorry, Poppy, that you and your sister didn't get parts in the play. I'm devastated. Seriously."

My mouth dropped open. I couldn't hide my shock. *I didn't get any part at all?*

I could feel my muscles tighten. My stomach suddenly churned. I didn't want to give Rose the satisfaction of seeing my dismay and how upset I was. But I couldn't help it.

Rose narrowed her eyes at me. She saw my surprise. She clapped a hand to her mouth. "Oh. I'm sorry," she said. "You hadn't heard?"

I shook my head.

She formed a pouty look on her face, puckering out her lips. "Wow. There I go again. Shooting off my big mouth. I thought you already got the word from Mr. G. I'm so sorry, Poppy."

Anger. Anger. Anger.

In that moment, I could write whole *books* of poems about anger. Was my face red? Was I trembling? I didn't care.

I lifted my backpack and dug my hand to the bottom. You're going to be very sorry, Rose. I found the knife

I keep in there. I wrapped my fingers around the handle, raised it quickly—and plunged the blade into Rose's stomach.

She gasped and drew back in pain.

"Oh, now I'm the one who's sorry," I said. "I'm so, so sorry, Rose. I thought that was the stage knife. The fake. But it isn't. Whoa. My mistake. I'm so, so sorry."

9

POPPY CONTINUES

Of course, that was a fantasy.

Can't blame a girl for her thoughts.

I had dinner at Ivy's house that night. Her parents had decided not to cook. We had a big bucket of fried chicken and a bunch of sides, and what could be better than that?

Didn't get me out of my funk, though.

After dinner, Jeremy and Manny joined us, and we went to my house. Heather wasn't home. No idea where she was.

Mom left a note saying she had to work late at her lab. Mom is an entomologist and studies insect control. She's doing some kind of experiments with hornets.

She explained it all to Heather and me a week or so ago. And she has to work fast because hornets don't have the world's greatest lifespan.

I grabbed tortilla chips and Cokes, and we huddled together in the den, all heavy green leather chairs and facing couches and a long dark wood coffee table cluttered with stacks of old magazines, and a fireplace we never use. The one room of the house designed by my dad before he and Mom split.

I was in the middle of describing my morning encounter with the lovely and talented Rose Groban. "She just let it slip that I didn't get a part in the play," I said.

Ivy's mouth dropped open. "No part at all?"

I nodded. "Sari Bakshi got Traci. And Kathy Taylor got Gretchen, the old lady. And Rose was gloating and grinning like her face would fall off."

I sighed. "I was so angry, I imagined a whole scene where I stabbed Rose in the stomach with a kitchen knife." I laughed. Not a ha-ha laugh, a bitter, inhaling laugh. "Believe it? I pictured myself pulling out a knife from my backpack and shoving it right into her gut."

"Are you sure you imagined it?" Manny said, grinning.

I rolled my eyes. "No. She's lying dead in a pool of

blood in the hall outside the home ec room."

"You've always had a good imagination," Ivy said. She smoothed a hand over her hair. Her eyes flashed. "Hey—maybe that could be our next prank. Murdering Rose!"

Manny laughed. "Our next prank? Who said we're going to do another prank?"

"Why not?" Jeremy chimed in. "Everyone loved the pet-store prank online. All those dogs going berserk. We are already up to fifty thousand views. We're famous!"

"So what can we do to Rose?" I said. "I'm serious about this. It's payback time. I want revenge. We've got to think of something." I shifted the navy-blue scarf around my neck. "Maybe I could just strangle her with this. You know. Keep it simple."

"Whoa, are you in a violent zone!" Ivy said. "You're scaring me, Poppy. Seriously."

"Okay," I said, "let's think of something nonviolent. Nonviolent but really mean and devastating that will ruin her life forever."

Manny laughed. "What's your problem? I think Rose is kind of hot."

I scowled at him. "You *would*." I heaved the tortilla-chip bag at his head. Missed, and it landed in his lap.

"Can we stick to the subject?" I said.

"What's the subject?" Jeremy asked. "Revenge against Rose for being Rose?"

"You got it," I said.

Ivy was perched on the wide leather arm of my chair. She jumped to her feet. "I know. We could go to the play and heckle her every time she comes onstage."

"That's not enough," I said. "And if we do that, if we heckle her, we'll just be thrown out of the auditorium. We'll look bad, we'll probably be suspended, and it'll make her happy."

Silence fell over the room as everyone tried to think of something. Actually, it wasn't silent. I could practically hear the hum of brains going into overdrive. Jeremy muttered to himself. Ivy had her eyes shut, concentrating. We all tried to come up with something really, really evil.

"Hey!" Jack's shout broke the silence. He burst into the room, his eyes going from person to person. Then he smiled—just for me. "Is this a wake? Everyone looks so serious."

"We're thinking," I said.

"Hey, Jack, do you have any more stray dogs in your truck?" Jeremy asked. "Maybe when the play starts, we could let them loose . . ."

Jack shook his head. "No stray dogs. I'm not working for the kennel anymore."

"We need something new," Ivy told Jeremy. "We can't repeat ourselves. That's too boring."

Jeremy shrugged. "Okay, I was just thinking."

Jack pulled Ivy off the arm of my chair and took her place. He squeezed my shoulder. A tender squeeze. No one was watching. I pressed my cheek against his hand.

"What are we thinking about?" he asked.

Ivy dropped onto the floor and rested her back against the couch. Manny shoved a handful of chips into his mouth and tossed the bag to Jack.

I had a flash. "Here's an idea," I said. "Rose keeps a water bottle on her dressing room table. She always has one. She drinks a lot of water. So—"

"You want to steal her water bottle?" Manny interrupted.

"No. What if we sneak in early and pour laxative in her water?"

"Whoa!" Manny jumped from his seat, clapping his hands.

Ivy tossed her head back and laughed. Jeremy stared at me as if he'd never seen me before.

"It's perfect," Manny said. "Ohmigod. And then she

walks onstage and . . . perfecto!"

"It's definitely mean enough," Jeremy said, still star-ing at me. I think he was shocked at what a devious mind I had.

"I love it," Ivy said. "If we can pull this off . . . awe-some idea, Poppy."

Jack was the only one who hadn't reacted. He climbed off the chair and strode to the fireplace. He leaned against the dark-wood mantel, shaking his head.

"What's wrong?" I said.

"You'll be caught," he said.

"Not if no one sees us do it," I argued.

"You'll be caught. Rose will know who did it. Every-one will know who did it. And the police—"

"Police?" I said, my voice getting shrill. "Why would the police care?"

"It would be considered an assault," Jack said. "You'd be arrested. Of *course* there'd be police."

I crossed my arms in front of me. "Fine. You don't like my idea? Okay, let's think some more."

I know. I sounded like a pouty, whiny five-year-old. But I was in an emotional state by this time. Maybe I was getting carried away. Maybe my idea was too horrible and humiliating.

I suddenly felt embarrassed.

We were silent for a long while, everyone thinking. And then . . . I had another idea. A smile slowly spread over my face. "Listen," I said. "Listen, guys. I've got a better idea. Let's cause a car wreck."

10

POPPY NARRATES

Ivy and Jeremy gasped. Manny's mouth dropped open and he nearly slid off his chair. "No way!" he cried. "No way! A real car crash?"

Jack laughed. "Awesome idea, Poppy. Get Rose in a car accident. Brilliant." I knew he was being sarcastic. He rolled his eyes. "Are you crazy?"

I shook my head. "No. You don't get it. No one actually gets in an accident. We *fake* a car wreck."

"I still don't get it," Manny said. He grabbed the bag of chips, reached inside. Empty. He crinkled it up and tossed it at me. "Try again, only this time, make sense."

"How do you fake a car wreck?" Jeremy asked.

"We don't want to hurt anyone," Ivy said. "Not even Rose."

"No one gets hurt," I said. "Let's say we do it an hour before the play is supposed to go on. Or maybe half an hour. We stage a big accident on Division Street, say, a block from the school."

"What good is that?" Jack demanded. "I really don't get this, Poppy."

I was becoming frustrated. My idea was awesome. I just was having trouble explaining it. "Don't you see?" I said. "We block all traffic to the school so no one can get to the play."

Silence while everyone thought about it.

Jeremy scratched his head. "You mean we block Division Street and Park Drive? More than one car?"

I nodded. "As many as it takes."

Manny squinted at me.

"We wreck our own cars?" Ivy asked.

"We don't *wreck* any cars," I replied. "We push our cars together in the middle of the intersection. We make it look like we had a collision. We all stand around and wait for the police and let the traffic back up for miles. Everyone trying to get to school for the play, only no one can get there." I gazed from face to face. "Don't you see? They'll have no audience. It's awesome, right?"

"Yeah. Maybe," Ivy said.

"If it works," Jeremy said.

"It could work," I said. "It could definitely work. Can you imagine Rose at school, waiting for the audience to pour in for the play, and no one shows up? Maybe a few people who walked there. But no one else. An empty auditorium. Can you imagine it?"

Jack laughed. "Yeah. I can imagine it. But it's dangerous, Poppy. What if the police figure out the accident is a fake?"

"Jack, I thought you liked danger," I teased.

He frowned. "I like danger, but I don't like getting caught."

"It might be genius," Manny said. "Is it a crime to fake an accident?"

"I don't think so," I said. "High school kids pull dumb stunts all the time, don't they?"

"Right," Manny agreed. "And when the cops show up and ask why none of the cars are even dented, we just say, 'Punked you!'"

"Yeah. We just say it was a typical high school joke," I said.

"Genius." Manny bumped knuckles with me. "And we can stream the whole thing, right?"

I nodded. "Yeah, for later. Maybe later that night. We put the video online after all the excitement dies down, and everyone will know it was another prank by us."

"I guess it's cool," Ivy said. She pulled her fingers through her long hair.

Everyone but Jack seemed to be getting on board.

"We'll have *two* pranks for our YouTube channel," Manny said. "The more pranks we pull, the more famous we'll get."

Ivy laughed. "We need a name for our group. Something to call ourselves, if we're going to be an outlaw prank group."

"How about the Outlaw Prank Group?" Jeremy suggested.

"That sucks," I said. "It doesn't sound cool at all. If we want to be famous—"

"How about the Prankers?" Ivy said.

Manny booed. "That's lame. What's a pranker? Sounds like a sore you get on your skin."

"No. That's called a *Manny*," Jeremy said.

We all laughed. Jeremy can be funny sometimes.

"I've got it," I said. "We'll be the Shadyside Shade. Because we're throwing shade on everyone."

"Love it," Ivy said. "Love it."

Jack nodded. "Yeah. I like it. The Shadyside Shade."

My phone vibrated. I glanced down at it. Keith calling. Keith, the forgotten man. Did I feel bad he wasn't here with my other friends? He wouldn't approve of our plan. He wouldn't approve of our name, our new group, our new YouTube plans. Keith would probably walk out of the house anyway. Or if he stayed, he'd try to discourage us.

I didn't take his call. I tucked the phone back into the armchair cushion.

"Are we at least going to try to make the accident look real?" Jeremy asked. "If we just have our cars touching in the middle of the intersection, it will totally look fake."

"But we can't really smash into each other," Ivy said. "My dad would slaughter me if I put even a tiny scratch on his new Subaru."

"We're not going to smash into each other," I said. "I think I have an awesome idea. Maybe—"

A door slammed, and I heard rapid footsteps. Heather walked into the room, hoisting a stack of books in front of her. She glanced quickly from face to face. "Hey, guys," she said, "what are you all talking about?"

I shot a look at each one of my friends. I didn't have to say it. We all knew for the prank to work, we had to be bound by silence.

"Not much," I said. "Just hanging out."

11

KEITH NARRATES

My chest is burning. Mom always makes everything too spicy for me. She likes hot sauce on everything, and she refuses to believe that I don't. I like shrimp and rice, but my mouth was on fire by the time I was halfway finished, and even a gallon of cold water didn't cool my tongue.

Of course, Jake, my ten-year-old brother, had to brag about how much he likes hot food, and he wolfed down the shrimp like it was candy, making faces at me the whole time, slobbering rice down his chin.

He doesn't know he's a total sitcom character, but he is. The little bro who acts so smart and superior and always competes with the older bro, and always WINS.

So why does *my life* have to be a sitcom?

Dad is sitting there shoveling in his dinner without even tasting it, as usual, giving Mom an endless account of how he installed some new refrigeration units at the box factory in Martinsville today. Dad is a hardworking dude, no question. But why does he think anyone at our dinner table is the tiniest bit interested in refrigeration units?

Meanwhile, my life is falling to pieces. And he's running on about how the cooling ducts didn't fit, and he had to change the compression gauges. Or something like that. I wasn't listening. I was watching Jake suck the burning hot shrimp down his greasy mouth with that crazy lopsided grin on his face.

Jake is cute. And he knows it.

He's just too much, you know? Always shouting, never speaking. Always pounding me every time he walks past. Too energetic, too all-over-the-place. I wasn't like that when I was his age. I was quiet. Studious. I have no idea how we ended up with him.

So now it's more than an hour later, and I guess I have what you call heartburn. Believe me, it's not the first time. Maybe it's from Mom's shrimp, or maybe it's from the stress, the aggravation that Poppy is causing me.

She's giving me the cold shoulder—the silent

treatment, literally ignoring me, shutting me out entirely. Do I deserve it? No way.

Well, okay, maybe I acted a little stuck-up about their pet-store riot. It turned out to be pretty funny, and no one got in trouble. Maybe I should have hung around, but I have to be careful.

Poppy doesn't understand the pressure I get from my parents. She knows I'm on the waiting list at Tufts. She knows I can't do anything to screw it up, or my dad will kill me. He had to drop out of Tufts to go into his family's refrigeration business, and now he's desperate for me to go there and finish.

If it doesn't work out, well, I'm kind of not sure what he'd do.

It puts a lot of stress on me. I'm not making excuses. Sometimes I'm *too* quiet and too cautious, and Poppy doesn't like it. I know that. But I can't change who I am. And I think she knows how much I care about her. I mean, it isn't easy for me to talk about things, but I've tried to tell her how much I care.

She's the first real girlfriend I've ever had, not counting the two weeks I went with Trisha-Lee in fourth grade. So . . . maybe I care too much. And maybe it hurts me too much when she doesn't want to hang out or she won't answer my texts and calls.

I know what she thinks. She thinks I'm this straight-arrow, no-fun guy. Especially since that strutting freak Jack showed up. But it's not true. I know how to relax and how to unwind and how to let loose. I know how to party.

It would be easier if I liked Poppy's friends. Ivy is so stuck-up, totally high on herself, waving her hair around and posing like she thinks she belongs in those gossip magazines she reads. She's pretty, but she's not as awesome as she thinks she is.

And Jeremy is just messed up. He can't pour ketchup on his cheeseburger without reading the ingredients on the bottle first. Like maybe he's allergic to tomatoes. I tried to bond with him—you know, connect in some way—but either he's off in a cloud or else he's so totally into himself and his problems, trying to talk with him is just . . . awkward.

Manny is fun. He's big and loud and funny, but we don't have much in common. I like to play *Madden Football*. I don't like *Call of Duty* or the other war games he's so obsessed with.

So my chest was burning. I was still burping up the spicy shrimp, and my head was kind of ringing, like a high, shrill whistle in my ears. I tried calling Poppy for the tenth time. And when I got her voicemail, I grabbed my dad's car keys, made my way out the back door without telling anyone, and backed his Mazda SUV, the one he bought used a few months ago, down the driveway.

Where was I headed? To Poppy's house, of course. It was a foggy night, not raining, but low clouds blocking the moon and the stars. I eased the car into drive and started to roll down the street. I had to make a hard stop when a family of raccoons came strolling across the street right in front of my car.

I counted at least six of them, two adults and four little ones, walking close together in a straight line, walking rapidly, silently, eyes straight ahead, as if the car headlights weren't even on them.

My heart was pounding. It got me a little shook. Because I almost ran over them. I might've rolled over all six at once, wiped out the entire family, and then I'd have to think about it for a long time, probably remember it for weeks. I guess maybe I'm oversensitive when it comes to that kind of thing.

Peering out into the fog, I drove slower than usual. I'm a careful driver, but I was super careful and cautious, and I made it to Poppy's house on River Road. She only lives fifteen minutes away. I slowed down, but I didn't stop. Because I recognized the pickup truck in her driveway.

Jack's truck. And then I spotted Ivy's mom's car parked at the curb, and then I could actually see them through the front window, Poppy and all her friends except me. I could see them all in the family room with that dark-green furniture.

I floored the gas pedal. The car lurched forward with a scream, like it didn't want to pull away but I was forcing it. The car screeched and I hoped they heard it inside the house. I hoped they heard it as I roared away, gripping the wheel but not really in control. Not really driving. Just shooting into the swirling wisps of fog, snakes of mist dancing in the light from my headlights.

The growl of the engine as I sped up River Road matched the roar in my head. Like we were one, the car and me. And I lost all caution, forgot about being so careful. I made my dad's car squeal into the turns as the road climbed, the river out of sight, lost in the fog far below. And I whipped around the curves like a thrill ride, a roller coaster at the state fair. Whipped around the curves, roaring and squealing, and man, did that feel good.

Too bad, Poppy. You're missing it. You're missing my

wild moment, my rocket trip through the fog, through space.

And when I pulled back up the driveway to my house, I didn't want the roaring to end. I didn't want the roar in my head to leave me. I needed it to drown out all the thoughts about Poppy. Poppy and her friends in her house, without me.

I could still feel the speed, the power of the car in my head. The house was dark. My parents had gone to bed. I walked to the liquor cabinet against the wall in the dining room, the floor tossing beneath my feet, shadows bouncing. Squinting into the dim light, I found the Jamaican rum.

That will do, I decided.

I grabbed a glass and carried the bottle to my room in the back of the house, tiptoeing on the wooden floorboards. I didn't want anyone to wake up and interrupt my night.

Sipping, sipping, feeling the warmth go down my throat, I stood staring out the window at the curtains of fog, shimmering gray against the purple night. Stood at my window, listening to the ocean crash inside my head, letting the liquid roll down my tongue. My chest burning even hotter now.

And then I walked to my desk and picked up the Swiss Army knife. Who gave me this knife? Was it a Christmas present from my great-aunt Clara?

I rolled up the sleeve of my T-shirt. I found the blade I like. Not too big, not too small, but sharp. The waves crashed in my skull, and I raised the blade to my shoulder and made a little cut.

Cut. Cut.

Not too deep. Just like before. Just like the other cuts crisscrossing my shoulder.

Cut. Cut.

Do you see, Poppy? Do you see?

You think you know so much, but I'm not what you think.

You've got me wrong.

You're so wrong. You don't know how wrong you are.

I made another cut, this one a little longer. Just an inch or two. I felt a warm trickle of blood. I felt the pain of the blade slicing so tenderly into my skin.

Cut. Cut.

It felt so good.

Just the right amount of pain.

12

POPPY NARRATES

Ivy was with me on the night of the school play. I sent Rose Groban a text: *Break a leg!* Simple but thoughtful. And then Ivy and I hurried to meet the others and cause a major car accident.

We were both giggly. Giddy. We both agreed it was going to be a hoot, a total riot. Neither one of us thought we could get in trouble. We drove in her mom's SUV, the radio blasting, Ivy thumping the dashboard with one hand as she drove. Me with my knees up on the glove compartment, so casual and relaxed.

We were a couple of blocks from school when Ivy broke the mood with a question. "Did you ever get around to breaking up with Keith?"

I nodded. "Well, yeah." Ivy sped up to make it

through a yellow light. "What made you think of him?"

She drove with one hand, tugged at her hair with the other. "I was just thinking how much he would *not* approve of what we're doing. The poor guy. He—"

"We don't have to worry about Keith anymore," I said. "I am out of the No Fun zone. I caught up with him at his job. You know, at his uncle's hardware store? And I just told him point-blank that it's over."

"Whoa." Ivy kept her eyes straight ahead as we pulled onto Division Street. "He probably guessed it was coming, right?"

"I'm not sure." I poked her with my elbow. "Watch out for that guy on the bike."

"I see him. What do you mean you're not sure?"

"Well, I think I saw tears in his eyes," I said.

Ivy's mouth dropped open. "OMG. He cried?"

"No. Just teared up," I said. "And went kind of pale. And then his lips got real tight. You know. Like he was holding himself in."

"And what did he say?"

"He didn't say a word. Just turned around and walked to the back of the store."

"The strong, silent type," Ivy said, slowing to let a woman with a baby stroller cross. "Do you think you broke his heart?"

"Who knows?" I replied. Her questions were starting to annoy me. Why did she have to know every detail? Did she have a thing for Keith? Not very likely. Ivy was always telling me to dump him.

"Keith is the most bottled-up person I ever knew," I said. "It was impossible to know what he was thinking."

"Well, he cared about you," Ivy said. "A lot."

"How do you know?" I snapped.

"Because he called me. To talk about you. He was worried you were going to break up with him."

"Enough about Keith," I said. I lowered my legs and sat up straight. "We're almost there. We've got to time this perfectly, right?"

The play's curtain was at eight. We planned to stage the accident at exactly seven fifteen. On a Saturday night there was a lot of traffic on Division Street. We had to make it look real. And we knew we'd have only one chance.

We had three cars. Ivy's, Jeremy's, and Jack's. Jack wasn't bringing the pickup truck. He'd borrowed an SUV from his cousin. Manny was riding with Jeremy. He was our photographer, and it was his job to get everything on video.

We planned to put the video on Snapchat and maybe Facebook, too. And we'd already set up our Shadyside

Shade YouTube channel. It was ready for uploading.

Of course, we would do that later, after we backed up traffic till eight o'clock and made sure the high school auditorium was empty for Rose and her play.

You have to give us credit. We went for it.

As for the police? Well . . . we just didn't think they would take it seriously. Maybe we weren't thinking clearly. Maybe we didn't *want* to think about any consequences that would spoil our fun.

Ivy and I both took deep breaths as she inched the car closer to the intersection. My heart was thudding so hard in my chest, I could barely breathe. Please let this go right. Please let this go as we planned. I gripped the dashboard with both hands as if we really were going to crash.

But, of course, we didn't. I could see Jack's SUV coming toward us on the other side of Division Street. He was driving into the sunlight, so his windshield was covered in gold. And Jeremy's car was in place. Manny was waving at us from the passenger seat. And—talk about perfect timing—there was a sudden break in the traffic. No one in view for at least a block or two.

We edged our cars into the intersection. Ivy let out an excited squeal. "I can't believe we are doing this!"

she cried, gripping the wheel with both hands, leaning forward in anticipation until her face was almost at the windshield. "This is so stupid, Poppy. This is so stupid!"

Her car bumped Jack's SUV. Head-on. Just a tap of bumpers. And then Jeremy's car slid in from the side until it bumped our back door on my side. A thump that made Ivy and me jump, harder than we expected.

And there we were, the three cars pressed together in the middle of the intersection. I scrambled out of the car and left my door open. My legs were shaking. I had to grab the side of the car to steady myself.

Ivy jumped out, squealing, pumping her fists in the air.

"You're not supposed to look happy!" Manny screamed. "You were just in an accident. Stop celebrating, Ivy!" He was already standing on the roof of Jack's SUV, his phone raised, recording the "terrible, tragic" accident.

"Looking good!" Jack said, strutting around the three cars. He pulled open the driver's door on Jeremy's car. Then he raised the hood. He grinned at me. "Look upset, everyone. Come on. Let's see some acting."

"Here come the cars," Jeremy said, pointing. And yes, a stream of cars was heading toward us from each direction. We stood looking at our cars, shaking our heads, muttering to ourselves as if we didn't know how this had happened and didn't know what to do next.

The horns started. Cars began to back up. A silver oil truck rolled up behind Ivy's car. It had nowhere to go. I glimpsed Manny on the car roof, videoing everything, moving his phone from one car to another, and capturing our distraught, confused faces.

A man in a blue work uniform climbed out of his car and hurried over to us. "Can I help?" he asked me.

I just shook my head.

The driver of the oil truck joined him, an old guy with a Chicago Cubs cap tilted over his forehead. The two of them muttered to each other, shaking their heads.

I heard sirens in the distance, growing louder. I turned and saw the backup of cars. It stretched for blocks now. No one could get past us. No one could turn around. And, of course, no one could get to the high school.

I had one surprise I hadn't told anyone about. My great idea for making our accident look like a real wreck.

I waited till no one was watching. Then I opened the trunk of Ivy's car and pulled out my surprise: a smoke machine I'd taken from the Drama Club supply cabinet.

A crowd had gathered around us. And the police sirens were louder now.

I cradled the machine in my arms and slid to the side of Ivy's car. I slipped it onto the back seat. I glanced around, suddenly panting like a dog, unable to catch my breath. Was I really doing this?

I glimpsed Manny on the roof of Jack's SUV. He had his phone aimed at Jack's car. So far, no one had seen me.

I pulled open the compartment between the two front seats and plugged in the smoke machine.

Then I turned the machine on. Backed out of the car. Left the door open. Stepped back . . . back.

A few seconds later, wisps of black smoke floated from Ivy's car. I heard screams and startled cries.

"Look out!" a woman screamed. "Get back! Get back!"

"The car could *blow*!" another woman cried.

"Smoke! Help! Smoke! It's going to *explode*!"

People were wide-eyed with fright, backing away. I couldn't keep a grin off my face. I hoped no one could see how pleased I was with my little smoke trick.

Ivy and I backed away, our eyes on the billowing black smoke. I squeezed Ivy's hand. I wanted to celebrate. We had pulled this crazy stunt off. The Shadyside Shade were in business, and we were going to be stars.

I thought of Rose in the auditorium, standing in a nearly empty theater, wondering why no one had come.

I thought of all the attention we were about to get, thousands of views online. *Thousands.*

I was thinking only good things when flames shot up from Ivy's back seat. The black smoke billowed even higher, and the bright yellow-orange flames leaped from the car.

Ivy's car.

I was still squeezing her hand as we watched, paralyzed, watched the flames grow wider, watched Ivy's car burn.

13

POPPY CONTINUES

Like a dream, what happened next didn't seem to take place in real time. Some of it came at me so fast, I couldn't take it in. And some of it was in painful slow motion so the unfolding horror had plenty of time to soak into my brain.

When the flames leaped from Ivy's car, I gripped her hand and stared as if I'd never seen flames before. I saw Jack reach up, grab Manny, and pull him from the roof of the SUV, where he was recording the whole scene. Manny fell, landed on his knees on the pavement, and Jack pulled him to his feet.

Then Jack and Manny were both screaming and gesturing frantically, "Run! Get away!" And I saw Jeremy, his eyes wide with fright, push himself off the side of his car and start to run.

Hypnotized by the darting flames, Ivy and I lingered— too long—and when the flames reached the gas tank and the car exploded with a deafening roar, we felt the heat on our backs as we were running after Jeremy. I opened my mouth in a shrill animal scream as the force of the explosion shoved me into Ivy, and we both went down.

Am I on fire?

The horrifying question forced out all other thought. I rolled on the pavement, forced myself to sit up—and realized I was unharmed. My back still burned from the heat of the explosion. My skin tingled. My heart pounded so hard, my chest ached. But I wasn't hurt.

Ivy and I helped each other up. We turned and watched the three cars burning. Flames rising high, clouds of black smoke curtaining the purple evening sky. The thunder-roar of the explosion fading in my ears, I began to hear the screams and shouts all around. And I saw the frightened faces as people ran from the burning cars, expecting another explosion.

"Here come the police." Jack was at my side now, pulling me across the street, my legs not cooperating, stumbling, stiff.

"Is everyone okay?" I screamed. "Is everyone okay? Is everyone okay?" I don't know how many times the cry escaped my throat. I couldn't stop. Until I saw Ivy and Jeremy and Manny at the side of the old oak tree, the fat, gnarled trunk so familiar. I must have passed it a thousand times on the way to school. So solid and real while the screams and shouts and pounding footsteps were all a dream taking place across the street.

Someone else's nightmare. No. *Ours*.

"Listen! Listen to me!" Jack desperately trying to corral us and get our attention. The flames were reflected on our faces, as if we carried them with us.

Jeremy leaned heavily against the tree trunk and lowered his head. He moaned. "I . . . feel sick."

"Listen to me! Listen to me!" Jack still trying. I was so dazed, his voice sounded a hundred miles away. I saw dark-uniformed police circling the cars, moving the crowd back. And the high drone of fire-truck sirens, rising and falling as they came into view.

"This wasn't a prank!" Jack screamed, trying to pull us together. I saw Jeremy being sick, hanging onto the tree trunk, turning his head away from us as he puked.

"Listen to me!" Jack was shaking Ivy by the shoulders, I guess trying to get the dazed-zombie expression off her face. Her hair was wild and tangled, but she made no attempt to straighten it.

All of us stood in wide-eyed disbelief, not talking, not looking at each other . . .

And this was my idea. This was all my fault.

I gazed at the crowd of people, the cars backed up along Division Street for miles. And a crazy thought flashed through my mind: *At least Rose is standing there at school with no one in the audience.*

Then I thought: dumb. Everything about this was dumb.

My idea . . . My idea . . .

And now, Jack, shaking his head, turned and crossed the street. I watched him step up to two police officers. They removed their caps and scratched their heads, almost in unison, as he talked with them.

A fire hose had been put into action. The flames were gone, and only the black smoke, the choking black smoke, remained, casting us in a dark fog. I could taste it, so bitter, on the back of my throat. Ivy began to cough. I pulled the scarf from around my neck and handed it to her to wrap around her mouth and nose.

Jack was gesturing to us, talking rapidly with the two officers. I waved a hand in front of my face, trying to clear a wisp of smoke away. Squinting across the street, I focused on Jack and the two cops. And I gasped when I thought I recognized the short, heavy one.

Was that the same cop who'd driven up beside me and stared at me from his patrol car?

"Oh, wow." I realized he kept turning his head from Jack and glancing at me.

Yes. The same cop who wouldn't answer me. Who'd just sat and stared. And now, here he came. He was trotting across the street toward us, his big stomach bobbing in front of him, his eyes on me.

Jack remained talking to the other officer. But this one was definitely coming for me.

What did he want?

What did he know?

14

POPPY NARRATES

My impulse was to run. I backed up until I bumped the trunk of the oak tree. Jeremy had his arm around Ivy's shoulders. Was she crying? I couldn't see her face.

I took a deep breath and readied myself to face the policeman.

He was short and round with his stomach bumping up against his uniform shirt. As he came up to me, I saw the big droplets of sweat on his broad forehead. His eyes were dark. He had a wide, almost flat nose, with an untrimmed black mustache beneath it. I lowered my eyes and saw that he had a hand on his gun holster as he trotted closer.

"Poppy?" His voice was surprisingly deep.

I nodded. *How does he know my name?*

He stopped, dark eyes locked on my face, and took a few seconds to catch his breath. Then he gestured to the smoldering cars with his cap, revealing dark, curly hair. "Never seen one like this," he said.

Was that suspicion in his eyes?

He shook his head. "How did it happen?"

I didn't know what to say. "It . . . just happened."

He nodded. I couldn't read his expression. Had he already figured out the truth? Was he waiting for me to tell him it had started out as a fake, a stupid prank?

The silence was awkward.

Finally, he said, "Do you know who I am? I'm Benny Kline. Manny's brother."

"Huh?" A startled sound escaped my open mouth.

"Manny has told me a lot about you," he said. He turned and motioned toward the cars, and I saw Manny beside Jack, talking to the other officer.

"I . . . I didn't know," I stammered. "I mean, I knew Manny had some older brothers. But I didn't know you were one. I mean . . ."

He laughed, a quiet laugh. "Manny talks about you all the time. You've been friends for a while, right?"

Cars were honking. Headlights flashed on as the sun

disappeared. The sky glared with red-and-blue lights from the circle of patrol cars. The black smoke had floated away, but the acrid smell remained. The police had convinced most of the crowd to return to their cars. But there was still nowhere for them to go.

"Yeah. Since eighth grade, I think." I started to relax. Manny's brother was just curious about me, I decided. He hadn't hurried over to accuse me.

"There are six of us," Benny said, tugging at his mustache. "Manny is the youngest. He's the only one still living at home. He was always the most trouble."

I blinked. "Trouble?"

"I'm kidding. Actually, all six of us were trouble. That's why I became a cop. To keep an eye on my other five brothers."

"Manny's a good guy," I said. "We have a lot of fun."

Benny's moustache drooped as his smile faded. "Well, this isn't much fun here tonight," he said, gesturing again to the ruined cars. "Hey, here come the tow trucks. We'll get this all cleared away quickly."

Ivy and Jeremy wandered over to us. Ivy still had that stunned expression on her face. Jeremy kept his arm around her. "I think Ivy may be in shock," he said.

"I can radio for some medics," Benny offered.

"No. No. Please," Ivy said. "I'll be okay. Really."

"Have you called your parents?" Benny asked. "You'd better call them right away. And, listen, take photos. Take a lot of photos before they clear the cars away. You know. For insurance."

A strange laugh burst from my throat. I covered it with a cough. Maybe I was in shock, too. I mean, this was supposed to be a joke, right? A fake accident to put online. And to keep everyone away from the play at school.

But now Division Street was insane with cops, and firefighters, and tow trucks, and our still-smoking, totaled cars, and angry drivers, and an ocean of other cars that couldn't move. And Benny was telling us what to do for the *insurance companies*?

A cold feeling swept down my body. None of this would have happened if I'd left the smoke machine in its closet at school.

The whole disaster was all on me!

And how long would it be before my friends would realize that the huge blaze was all my fault? How long before my friends confronted me about it? Or turned against me? Or . . . Or . . .

My eyes darted from one to another. Jeremy standing

with his arm around Ivy, talking to her softly, her whole body trembling, her cheeks tearstained. Manny with Jack, talking to some officers, gesturing wildly with their hands. I knew they had to be lying about how the accident had happened. I couldn't tell if the cops believed them or not.

It seemed so unlikely that three friends in separate cars would have an accident. So unbelievable. I mean, if I were a cop, would *I* believe it could be an accident?

Suddenly, I found myself thinking about Keith. Quiet, safe, boring Keith. He would never find himself in a mess like this. He would never agree to be part of something so insane. I knew there were more urgent things to think about. But there I was, asking myself, *Did I make a mistake by breaking up with Keith?*

Then I watched Jack trotting over to us, his eyes on me, his walk as confident as ever, his expression calm, as if this were just a minor setback, nothing to lose your cool over. And I knew I'd made the right choice.

He gave me a quick hug. "Are you okay?"

I nodded. "I guess."

Jack turned to the others, who had gathered around. Manny still gripping his phone. Jeremy with a protective hand on Ivy's shoulder. Jeremy shook his head. "We blew it."

"Could this be any more stupid?" Ivy said in a trembling voice. "I don't think so."

Jack gestured with both hands for everyone to calm down. "You're right. You're right," he said softly. The red-and-blue patrol car lights reflected off his face.

"I'm sorry," I said, shaking my head. "I'm so sorry. Really." My breath caught in my throat. "No more pranks."

"No more pranks," Ivy repeated.

"No more pranks," Jeremy echoed.

We were all agreed.

But there was one more prank to come. One more prank . . . The most dangerous and devastating of them all.

15

IVY CONTINUES THE STORY

"I had to shampoo my hair three times, and I still can't get rid of the smoke smell. It's totally gross."

I was in my room, a towel wrapped around my wet hair, stretched out on my back, fiddling with the belt on my bathrobe and talking with Poppy, who had called to share horror stories about having to confess to our parents.

She has only one parent. Her father is completely out of the picture, as far as I can tell. So I think that makes it easier for her.

When I phoned my parents and they came rushing to Division Street to see the smoldering remains of their car, they hugged and kissed me. Mom wiped away tears. They repeated again and again how relieved they were that I was okay.

Then they took turns saying how they would never be able to trust me again for the rest of my life. And they instantly teamed up in finding suitable punishments that would pretty much ruin every day of my life for at least my remaining days in high school.

"Listen, I can't talk long," I said. "My parents are downstairs waiting for me for another family conference. They're busy dreaming up more ways to make my life a horror story."

"My mom was very understanding," Poppy said. Her words made me cringe. *Understanding?*

"Of course she was understanding!" I cried. "It wasn't your car. We didn't use your car—remember? Instead, we blew up *my* car."

Silence at her end for a moment. Then, "Ivy, you don't have to shout. You know I feel terrible—"

"*How* terrible?" I snapped. I could feel the anger burning through me. It started in my chest, a red-hot feeling that tightened my muscles as it traveled over my whole body.

I sat up straight. I felt like *I* was about to explode. Like my car. Waves of black smoke would come pouring out over my room.

I tried to hold myself back. I tried to fight the red anger down, but it was even in my eyes now. Poppy was my best friend. But I had to say it. I couldn't hold it in.

"It was *your fault*, Poppy." The words tumbled from my mouth.

"Ivy, wait—" she started.

But it was too late. Too late. "The smoke machine," I said. "The smoke machine. *What were you thinking?*"

"I—I—" She could only stammer.

"You didn't offer *your* car," I shouted. "We took my car instead."

"I know, but—"

"But what?"

"Ivy, you're blaming me for everything?" Poppy's voice caught on the words. I could hear that she was hurt, but at that moment, I didn't care. I had to get it all out.

"No," I said. "It's Jack, too. If you hadn't brought him around . . . If you hadn't made him part of the group . . ."

"Then what?" I could hear her getting angry, too.

"Then we wouldn't be in this mess."

"Listen, Ivy, you can blame me all you want. But you can't blame Jack. I'm the one who wanted to teach Rose Groban a lesson. I'm the one who wanted to do something bad to Rose. It wasn't Jack's idea. It was mine."

"He doesn't belong in our group, Poppy." I regretted the words as soon as I'd said them. I think I believed them, but I knew instantly it was a terrible thing to say.

"Jack doesn't *belong in our group*?" Poppy's voice went high and shrill. "Why? Because he's fun?"

I took a breath. "No. Because he's trouble." With one hand, I rearranged the towel over my hair. I really had to get off the phone and dry it properly. This conversation had already gone on for too long. Way too long.

I wished I could rewind it and take out what I'd said about Jack. Because now Poppy was furious at me and even more upset than when she had called, which was plenty upset.

And now I was completely confused. Was I really angry at Poppy? Or was I just exploding because the whole night had gone so wrong and I was in so much trouble?

"Go ahead, blame me," Poppy said, lowering her voice to a growl. "I can see you want to blame somebody. Well, fine. Blame me. The smoke machine . . . the revenge against Rose . . . using your car . . . it was all my idea. Blame me."

"I . . . I'm sorry," I said. "Listen, my parents are waiting downstairs to give me twenty lashes with a bullwhip and then boil me in oil. So I've got to go. Let's talk tomorrow, okay?"

Silence.

"Okay?"

"Good luck with your parents," she said coldly. Then clicked off.

I sat there, suddenly numb. I didn't want to lose Poppy as a friend. We'd shared too many good times together. I never should have mentioned Jack.

The room was spinning around me. I had the feeling that I was on a merry-go-round, and it was going too fast for me to jump off.

I stood up, holding onto the bedpost, and waited for the room to stop twirling. I started to the hall. Might as well face my parents and get it over with.

But as I stepped out of my room, my phone dinged. I raised it to my face and stared at the text message that had just appeared. Blinking, I read it twice. I gripped the phone hard to keep it from slipping from my hand. And then I cried out: "Manny did *what*?"

16

KEITH NARRATES

I sat in my car and watched the video on my phone. I actually screamed when the flames burst from the back of Ivy's car, and then I just sat there with my mouth open, unable to react when the car exploded in a burst of black smoke.

I couldn't believe Manny had recorded the whole thing. And I couldn't believe he put it online for everyone in the world to see. Mainly because it looked like a stunt. It didn't look like an accident. And if the police and other people started to figure out this was fake, just a prank that went wrong, my friends could be in major trouble. I mean, my former friends, of course.

Poppy wasn't speaking to me. She just ignored me

in the halls at school. I didn't know what I had done to deserve it. After all, she broke up with me. I didn't dump her. I tried hanging with Jeremy and Ivy, but they acted really awkward around me. And I never really liked them much anyway. So . . . forget them.

And now I was watching another dumb prank they had pulled. This one blew up in their faces, literally, and I was glad not to have been there, glad not to be part of that group of idiots and their stupid jokes.

And could there be anything more stupid than putting the whole thing online? What was Manny thinking?

Whoa. No way. Now the street was filled with cops and firefighters, and everyone was out of their cars just gawking and shaking their heads. And there were Ivy and Poppy looking so sad, as if they were totally innocent and had no idea how the whole thing could have happened.

I had thought Poppy and I were a good couple. I was really into her. I mean really. And when she dumped me for that clown, Jack, I guess I went a little crazy. I went into fantasyland for a while.

I never told anyone, but I kept imagining her coming after me and begging me to take her back.

I had whole long conversations in my mind with

Poppy crying and pleading and telling me how awesome I was and how dumb she was to be attracted to Jack, even for a minute. Sometimes in my imagination, we made up, and we wrapped our arms around each other, and I actually had a real warm feeling from it.

But other times, I resisted her. I was smart. She had proven she was not a good person. She was too wild and impulsive and thoughtless and cruel. And in my imaginary talks with her I told her to go away. I told her I could never care about someone like her, someone who would throw me away like a piece of trash.

I watched part of Manny's video again. Then I tossed my phone onto the passenger seat and drove toward River Road. No, I hadn't planned to go by Poppy's house. That's just the direction I chose. I didn't really know where I was going.

I wished I had someone to share the video with, someone to laugh about it with and talk to about how dumb everyone was. But I didn't. I was alone. And I ended up at Harlow's Pic 'n' Pay just before River Road starts to curve up from the river. Sometimes Harlow lets me buy a beer without carding me. He's a good old guy.

I parked in the little lot in back and stepped in through the back door. It took a few seconds for my eyes to adjust to the lights. Harlow keeps the store extra-bright because he thinks it will discourage robbers. Good luck with that.

He was behind the glass counter in front pulling up some lottery tickets for an old couple. I started toward the beer fridges and bumped into a tall, skinny guy with a floor mop and bucket.

"Hey—" My eyes were still adjusting, and I almost didn't see him.

He had greasy brown hair down over his forehead and funny eyes, dark eyes that seemed to be darting around all the time, like they were nervous. He had a silver ring in one ear and a silvery nose ring, and he wore a plain sleeveless white T-shirt over low, baggy jeans that looked like they'd drop to the floor at any second.

"How's it going?" he said, leaning on the mop handle.

"Not bad." I realized I'd seen him before. "You go to Shadyside?"

He shook his head. "Dropped out last year. Couldn't take any more. You know?"

I tried to edge past him, but the soapy bucket was in the way. "So you work here?" I asked.

"Yeah. And a couple other places. Maintenance work. You know."

"Maintenance work?"

"Yeah. I mop up and stuff. I'm Lucas. Lucas Smith."

"Keith Carter," I said.

I glanced to Mr. Harlow at the front. He was just shooting the breeze with the old couple while they scratched off their tickets. I turned back to Lucas. "Do you think I could get a beer?"

He propped the mop against the wall. "Yeah. No problem. I'll get you one." He motioned with his head to a small back room. I stepped inside. It was narrow and dimly lit. Stacks of soda and beer cases on one wall. Shelves of cleaning supplies.

Lucas brought me a Bud and I twisted off the cap. "Thanks, man." I dropped onto a narrow wooden stool and took a long sip. It felt good on my throat. I hadn't realized how much I needed it.

Poppy suddenly flashed into my mind. I don't know why she kept showing up in my thoughts. I chuckled, thinking about how shocked she would be to see me drinking a beer.

She didn't know me at all. And she didn't care enough to find out.

I took another long slug of the Bud. Lucas and I talked for a while. He'd dropped out of school last year because his dad had left, and his family needed the money. He now did janitor-like work in three or four stores, and he said it paid him enough to get by.

He pulled a cigarette from a crinkled pack and offered the pack to me. "Smoke?"

I shook my head. "No. I don't."

He lit it with a plastic lighter and took a long drag. "You should. It's very relaxing. Seriously."

I watched him take another long puff. The smoke curled around his face. "You know they're not good for you, right?" I said.

He snickered. "Doctors don't know everything."

I shrugged. "Whatever." I finished my beer, thanked him, and climbed to my feet. I stopped at the doorway to the little back room. "What do you do for fun?" I asked him.

The question made him blush. His cheeks turned bright pink. A strange, lopsided smile spread across his face. "I like to follow girls around the store," he said. "You know. I'm a stalker." And then he burst out laughing. This crazy laugh. It just erupted from his chest.

I thought he was joking. I couldn't really tell. So I just ignored what he said. Maybe I should have taken him seriously. I don't know. Maybe I should have warned someone about him.

Later, in my room with the door locked, I cut a little deeper than usual. The knife dug into my shoulder. But I didn't feel it at all. I was pretending to cut Poppy.

Cut cut.

It was *her* that I wanted to hurt.

17

POPPY CONTINUES THE STORY

"Do you want fries with that?"

The guy pretended to think about it. I knew him and his friend from school. They're on the Shadyside Tigers basketball team and they think they're hot stuff. Wilson Teague and LeShaun Jenks. Actually, they *are* hot stuff.

"Can I have onion rings instead?" LeShaun asked, waving the menu at me.

I nodded. "Okay."

Wilson grinned up at me. "Can I have half fries, half onion rings?"

No way Lefty would do that. I grabbed the menu from him. "You're pulling my chain, right?"

They both laughed.

I saw Ivy and Jeremy walk into the restaurant. They took a booth near the kitchen. I started away from the table, then turned back to the two guys. "I forgot. How do you want your cheeseburgers?"

"Cooked?"

"On a plate?"

I frowned at them. "You guys are a riot."

They both laughed again. "You're looking good, Poppy," Wilson said. "You still hanging with Keith?"

"Keith is history," I said. I saw Lefty watching me from the kitchen. Waitresses weren't supposed to have conversations at the tables. Lefty had listed all his rules for me when I'd started two days before. It was a pretty long list. I remembered most of them, I thought.

Lefty pounded the bell on the counter. That meant there were cheeseburger plates ready to be picked up. I tore the guys' order off my pad and handed it to Lefty. Then I hurried to deliver the plates.

Kat Martin, the other waitress on the early evening shift, had called in sick. So I was doing the whole restaurant. It wasn't a hard job, but it kept me moving nonstop.

It was cool in the restaurant. Lefty already had the air-conditioner going, even though it was only April. But I kept mopping beads of sweat off my forehead with the back of my hand. And the black-and-yellow cap with the big *L* on the front that Lefty makes us wear as part of our uniform was making my hair itch.

I took orders at two more tables and refilled water glasses around the room. Then I walked over to Ivy and Jeremy's booth. They were holding hands across the tabletop and, for a brief moment, I felt a pang—of loneliness, I guess.

Jack hadn't been around much. We texted each other, and he called once to tell me about something he was scheming. But since the car accident disaster, he had made himself pretty scarce.

"Poppy, tell me again why you're working here?" Ivy said, letting go of Jeremy's hands.

"Because I love cheeseburgers," I said. She knew perfectly well why I had to take this job. After the car prank, Mom had said I had to have an after-school job to show that I could be a responsible person. She said I had to keep the job all summer. So here I was, a block from school, waitressing at the home of the two-dollar double cheeseburger.

Ivy sighed. "You got off easy, you know. My parents aren't letting me take that modeling course in New York. They made me call them up and cancel it. I have to stay in Shadyside and be a nanny to my two cousins in North Hills."

"Oh, wow," I murmured. "That's harsh."

Ivy's eyes teared up. "My life is ruined, and all because of a bad joke."

"I had an internship lined up at the summer theater at the Town Center," I said.

I didn't want Ivy to think that she was the only one whose life was ruined. I guess I'm more competitive than I thought. Or maybe I just wanted to share the misery around.

I turned to Jeremy. "You haven't said a word."

He shrugged. "I had an allergy shot this morning, and I'm feeling kind of weird."

Lefty rang the bell. I saw Wilson's and LeShaun's food on the counter. I carried it to them and wrote out a check for the table behind theirs. Then I came back to Ivy and Jeremy.

"Can you two come to my house when my shift is over? Jack said he'd come by because he has something to talk to us about."

"Oh, no. Not another prank," Jeremy said, shaking his head.

"Don't you think it's a little soon?" Ivy said. "Maybe

we should slack off for a while. Like maybe twenty years or so?"

"I know where you're coming from," I said. "But Jack says he has an awesome idea that *can't* go bad."

Ivy and Jeremy both started talking at once, but I didn't hear them. My eyes were on the restaurant door, where two girls had just walked in. The bright sunlight through the glass door kept me from recognizing them immediately. But then my eyes focused and I saw Rose Groban looking around for an empty table. And standing beside her . . . my sister?

"What is Heather doing with Rose?"

Ivy and Jeremy both turned to look at them. I hadn't realized I'd said those words out loud. Lefty was pounding the bell, but I couldn't stop staring at the two of them.

They sat down across from each other at the table closest to the door. Rose wore a long-sleeved top, a bright magenta color, over a short black skirt. My sister was drab as usual, in a red-and-gray Shadyside High jersey and jeans with ragged holes at both knees. I recognized the blue flip-flops she kept kicking the table legs with. They were mine.

"They don't usually hang together, do they?" Ivy said.

"Not usually," I replied. "See you two later?" I didn't wait for an answer. I turned and made my way to the front booth.

Has Heather made a new friend?

She knows how much I detest Rose.

What is she plotting?

I couldn't keep the questions from whirring in my mind as I stepped up to them. But I took a breath and forced myself to play it cool. "Hey, what's up?"

Rose forced a smile. "Hey, Poppy."

I stared at Heather. She knew I needed an explanation.

"Rose is giving me acting lessons," she announced. "She thinks I show promise."

Rose grinned at me, flashing her perfect teeth. "Maybe you'd like to join us. We could have our own acting seminar."

"I don't think so," I said quietly.

"But that could be so much fun," Rose gushed. "And we could really give Heather a tutorial on everything we've learned."

I kept myself from strangling her. "I'm kind of busy," I muttered.

Of course, I knew what was going on here. Rose was

trying to make me look like a bad sister. But come on. No way I'd encourage Heather to join the Drama Club. She had no talent. Not the tiniest spark. So Rose was stepping right in and giving Heather the attention and the support she couldn't get from me.

Rose still had that phony smile on her face. "You look awesome, Poppy," she said. "That uniform suits you. Seriously. The black and the yellow . . . The yellow really brings out your features."

Nasty. But I wasn't going to fall into any trap. I just gave her a fake smile back. "How was the play, Rose?" Of course, I knew the answer.

"Unfortunately, we had to postpone it," Rose said. "But we're going to perform it for the whole school in a few weeks, so you'll get to see it." She and Heather shared a glance. "It was postponed because of your accident," Rose said. "Did they ever figure out whose fault it was?"

I shook my head. "It wasn't anyone's fault. It was just an accident."

Rose put her hands together, like she was praying. "Poppy, I'm just so grateful you weren't hurt."

What a laugh.

Heather kept this solemn look on her face, as if she believed Rose was being sincere. I wanted to puke. Really.

I raised my pad. "What can I get you?"

They ordered double cheeseburgers. Rose asked for hers to be rare. And Heather asked for rare, too. I squinted at her. She had never wanted a rare burger before in her life. Was she just trying to impress Rose? How pitiful was that?

I put in their order. I took care of a couple of other tables. All the while, I kept my eyes on Rose and Heather. They were laughing together, both talking at once, both very animated and enthusiastic. As if they were best buds.

It was all so clear. Rose was trying to grab my sister away. Another round in this endless competition she and I had. And then, of course, she'd act totally innocent and naive and pretend she didn't know what any of the fuss was about.

And poor Heather. My sister was so desperate for attention, I could see she was eating this up. Her normally sickly pale skin was pink and vibrant, and her dull, almost colorless eyes were actually alive behind her glasses.

So totally sad.

I could feel the anger burning my chest. This was such a Rose move. And I knew that when she got bored playing this game, she would drop Heather in a heartbeat.

Oh, well. What could *I* do about it? I could imagine the furious reaction I'd get from Heather if I told her that Rose was only using her to get to me. I knew that would be a mistake, a mistake that could lead to World War III between us.

The bell rang, startling me. I was standing right in front of the counter. I picked up the two plates with the rare cheeseburgers and carried them across the restaurant to Rose and Heather.

They were giggling together about something but stopped when I approached. Heather had a guilty smile on her face. She knew she was hanging with Rose just to mess with me.

I was determined to show her that I didn't care at all. Whatever. Heather thought she had a great victory over me right now, but it couldn't be a victory if I didn't play along—if I didn't get angry.

My problem is, I have a totally obvious face. Whatever I'm feeling or thinking shows up there instantly.

I was seriously steamed that Heather would pull this kind of stunt. The anger was just bubbling hot inside me.

But I gritted my teeth, stepped up to their table and set the plates down. "Here you go. Anything else I can get you?"

Heather kept her eyes on Rose. Rose stared down at her cheeseburger. When she finally raised her eyes, her mouth was twisted in a scowl.

"Anything wrong?" I asked. I could hear my voice go shrill.

"I asked for mine without a bun," Rose said.

"Huh?" I gaped at her. "No, you didn't."

"Yes, I did," she insisted. "I said rare with no bun."

I could feel all the muscles in my body tightening. "I didn't hear that." I turned to my sister. "Did you hear her say no bun?"

Heather blushed. "I don't remember."

She's useless.

I could see Lefty watching me from behind the counter. I turned back to Rose. "Well, just remove the bun, Rose. Take it off."

She brushed back her hair. "I don't want to do that. I asked for no bun."

"But, Rose—"

"If a bun is on the plate, I'll be tempted to eat it," Rose said.

My heart was suddenly pounding. Was I really having this discussion? Anyone else in the world would simply remove the cheeseburger from the bun and not even think of making a fuss about it.

"I don't mean to be difficult," she said, "but can you take it back and bring me one without the bun?"

"I can do better than that," I said in a tight voice I barely recognized. I reached down to her plate and removed the top half of the bun from her cheeseburger. I placed the top half on the table. Then I picked up the cheeseburger from the bottom and smashed it as hard as I could into her face.

18

POPPY CONTINUES

I pushed hard, watching the cheese spread over her cheeks. The tomato slid down the top of her magenta shirt, and when I pulled my hand back, the rest of the cheeseburger plopped onto her lap.

Rose didn't react at first. Then her eyes bulged and her mouth opened wide, and she let out a shrill, angry scream that sounded like the wail of an ambulance siren.

Everyone in the restaurant turned to watch as she bolted up from her seat and, still screaming, wrapped her hands around my throat, and tried to pull me over the table.

Heather was screaming now and struggling to get out of her seat as the table came crashing down, plates and glasses clattering, water puddling. Rose and I landed on top of it. She still had her stranglehold on my neck, and I was struggling to shove her arms away. We were wrestling and squirming over each other. The shouts of customers in the restaurant drowned out my groans and cries of pain.

And then Lefty's voice broke through the noise. He was standing in the middle of the restaurant, his head tilted to one side like a parrot, his chef's cap in one hand, waving a metal spatula in the other.

Then he gathered a breath and bellowed in a tone I did not know he possessed, "Poppy!"

Everything froze. Everything and everyone. And the big room grew silent. Rose's fingers slipped from my throat, and she fell back onto the floor and seemed to deflate like a balloon losing its air.

Lefty pointed the spatula at me. "Can I see you for a minute?"

Gasping for breath, I scrambled off Rose and turned to Lefty. "Am I—am I fired?"

Lefty narrowed his eyes at me. "Three guesses."

"Rose is ruining my life," I moaned. "I know what you're going to say. She and I have been enemies since time began. But now it's different."

Manny had his flip-flops off, bare feet on the coffee table. He leaned back in the big leather armchair and laughed. "Poppy, I didn't know you were training for the WWE. You and Rose! A steel-cage match. We could take bets. Maybe put it on our YouTube channel."

I was on the couch across from Manny. I kicked his feet. "You're about as funny as stomach cramps. I'm being serious here. She tried to strangle me. Look at my neck. You can see her fingerprints on my skin."

"I think maybe you started it," Jeremy said. He and Ivy sat cross-legged on the carpet at the other end of the couch. "You know. Shoving a cheeseburger into her face."

"I had no choice," I said. "It had to be done."

Jack came in from the kitchen carrying two cans of Coke. He handed me one and dropped down beside me. "It's a violent world," he said, shaking his head. "I blame the rap music and video games."

"Give me a break, Jack." I shoved him. "You're about as funny as Manny." I jumped to my feet. "Are you all with me or not? Rose has declared total war!"

Ivy climbed to her feet. She stumbled over Jeremy's legs as she walked over to me. She wrapped me in a hug.

"We're with you, Poppy," she said softly. "I've never seen you like this. I'm really sorry this happened to you, and we . . ."

Blah, blah. I only half-heard what Ivy was saying. My thoughts were swirling in my head, spinning like a merry-go-round gone berserk. "My own sister is on her side," I moaned.

"Heather was just trying to push your buttons," Jeremy said. "That's what sisters are for, right?"

"Wrong," Ivy said. "Heather knows the score. She knows how Poppy and Rose feel about each other."

"Heather has a lot of anger," I said. I dropped back down beside Jack. "You're being quiet," I told him.

"I'm thinking," he said. He was tossing his car keys from hand to hand. The can of Coke was tucked between his knees. He hadn't touched it.

"Aren't we the Shadyside Shade?" I said, feeling a surge of energy. "Forget about Rose Groban. Come on, guys. Help me forget about her and my sister and everything. Let's do something wild."

Ivy curled and uncurled a strand of hair. "I don't think so," she said. "That last prank ruined my whole life, Poppy. No New York. No modeling course. Nothing. I say forget the Shadyside Shade."

Jack finally spoke up. "Unless we have an awesome idea. And I've got one."

Jeremy rolled his eyes. "We're all in so much trouble, we may not survive high school. We should never pull another prank again."

Jack shook his head. "But we're famous, Jeremy. We have tons of followers. They're waiting for our next stunt." A thin smile crossed his face. "And I have a good one."

I gave him another shove. "Enough introduction. Stop keeping us in suspense. What's your big idea?"

"We go rogue!" Jack said.

I squinted at him. "Huh? What does *that* mean?"

"We go outlaw!" he exclaimed.

"Jack, what are you talking about?" Ivy demanded.

His silvery eyes flashed. "We rob a store."

19

HEATHER TAKES OVER THE STORY

"Does your nose still hurt?" I asked. "I don't see a bruise."

Rose moved the hand mirror to a different angle and narrowed her eyes, examining her skin. "She could have broken it," she muttered through gritted teeth.

"My sister is crazy," I said, shaking my head. "She's not usually a violent person, but she's angry. Especially when it comes to me." I sighed. "Don't ask me why."

We were in Rose's bedroom, perched on the edge of the peach-colored quilt over her bed.

I had a large paper cup of iced tea in my hand. I took a long sip as I watched Rose. She lowered the mirror to her lap and patted her skin tenderly with the palm of one hand.

"If she had broken my nose, I'd have no choice, Heather. I'd have to sue. And there's no way I could lose. Poppy assaulted me, and there are at least a dozen witnesses. Everyone in that restaurant saw what she did."

"Insane," I muttered. "Totally insane." I didn't know what else to say.

My first time hanging with Rose. My first opportunity to learn about acting. The first person who ever took me seriously, who offered to be a friend and help me and teach me. And what does Poppy do? She spoils the whole thing. Deliberately tries to spoil my chance.

Why? Jealousy? That can't be right. Poppy can't be jealous of me. She has the awesome looks and the good friends and the sparkly personality. She has everything I wish I had. So . . . it can't be jealousy.

Does she just plain hate me? She has no reason to hate me. I've always wanted to be close to her. I've never done anything to hurt her.

What is her problem?

"Of course, I wouldn't really sue," Rose said, crossing to her dressing table. She sat down and began to rearrange her hair.

She's so beautiful. She could be an actress. She seriously has the looks. "Poppy and I have known each other for too long," she continued, looking at me in the mirror. "I couldn't sue her or your family. I always considered her a friend."

She began to run a hairbrush slowly through her hair. "Sure, we have our competitive sides, but that's just fun. It's fun to test each other, to try to win against one another in school or in Drama Club or wherever. I never took it seriously."

I didn't reply. I knew Poppy took it *very* seriously.

"It's not like we're archenemies or something," Rose said, brushing faster.

Oh, yes, it is.

And of course *that* explained why Poppy had gone berserk. She saw me sitting there enjoying myself with her archenemy. The whole thing was about me. I guess I should have been flattered, flattered that my sister cared so much.

But . . . no way. I'm entitled to my own life and my own friends. She will never share her friends with me. Never. She always shuts me out. So what gives her the right to decide who I hang out with?

"Your sister didn't just try to humiliate me," Rose said, setting down the hairbrush and turning her head to admire her work in the mirror. "She tried to hurt me. But I know she'll do the right thing and apologize."

"I'm not so sure," I said. "I know her and her temper. Also, it cost her her job. She's probably waiting for *you* to apologize."

Rose grinned. "Yes. Definitely. It was my fault for putting my face in front of the cheeseburger."

We both laughed.

I finished the iced tea and turned the cup in my hands. Rose crossed to her desk and rifled through a stack of papers. "Let's give you your first acting lesson," she said. She handed me a one-page script. "We'll start with the best. See how you do."

I skimmed through the lines quickly. "What is this? Shakespeare?"

She nodded. "Did you read *Macbeth* in ninth grade?"

"Yes. But I didn't understand a lot of it. I thought—"

"It's Lady Macbeth's soliloquy. Remember it?"

"Not really." I squinted up at her. "You really want me to start with Shakespeare? Shouldn't we try something easier?" I tried to read the first lines.

"'They met me in the day of success, and I have learned by the perfect'st report they have more in them than mortal knowledge. When I burned in desire to question them further, they made themselves air, into which they vanished.'"

"Rose? What does that mean?"

An indulgent smile crossed her face. It was the kind of smile you give an infant. "You need to go slow and think about it and work at it, Heather. Take one line at a time. Go over it until you know the words and the meaning."

I stared at the words. They were all a blur now. "Do you have a script to the play you're doing at school?"

She shook her head. "Trust me. Before you can do something easy, you need to try something hard."

Did that make sense? I decided I'd have to think about it. But I was thrilled that she wanted to pay so much attention to me. She must have thought I really had a spark of talent.

"Okay, I'll give it a try," I said. "I'll—"

Her phone buzzed and vibrated, interrupting us. She dove for it on the other side of the bed, glimpsed at the screen, and raised it to her ear. "Oh, hi. I wasn't expecting to hear from you."

I could hear a guy's voice on the other end.

"Wait a sec," Rose said into the phone. "Just a moment." She turned to me. "You'd better go now, Heather. I have to take this."

I nodded. And then the words blurted from my mouth: "You have a boyfriend?"

I saw a flash of anger in her eyes. Anger that I asked a question she didn't want to answer? She didn't reply at all. Just waited for me to get off the bed and leave.

But then I saw that her gaze was down at my hands. "Heather, look what you did," she said. "You scratched the backs of your hands. Look—you're bleeding."

I uttered a cry of surprise and stared at my blood-stained hands. "I did? Wow. I didn't even realize."

20

POPPY NARRATES

"Don't all jump in at once," Jack said. "You're staring at me like I'm speaking Martian. I said, let's rob a store."

"For real?" Ivy demanded. "Rob a store for real?"

"And video it?" I said. "So the police would know who to arrest?" I rolled my eyes. "That's *genius*!"

Jack scratched the side of his face. "Very funny. I thought you wanted to do something crazy."

I squinted at him as if seeing him for the first time. "Not that crazy."

Manny laughed. "I'm not sure my brother the cop will approve. He didn't like our dog-store prank at the mall!"

"I think we'd look awesome in those orange prison uniforms," Jeremy said.

Jack jumped to his feet. He had an impatient scowl on his face. I hadn't known him for long, but I'd already learned that sometimes he had a short fuse. He definitely didn't like being teased.

"Come on, guys," he pleaded. "It wouldn't be a real robbery. Just a prank. A fake. No one goes to prison for a prank."

"We do a fake robbery?" Ivy said. "But at a real store?"

Jack nodded. "We'll set the whole thing up but make it look totally real. You know. Like a reality TV show."

"And do we really take stuff?" Manny asked. "We could rob a shoe store. I need new sneakers. Look at these. They're, like, air-conditioned. I got so many holes in them."

Jack frowned at him. "That might be considered a real robbery, you know?"

"I know where you got this idea," Jeremy chimed in. He had been watching the whole discussion in near silence. I could see that Ivy was reluctant. But I hadn't been able to tell if Jeremy was into the idea or horrified by it.

"You saw the same video?" Jack asked him.

Jeremy nodded. "On YouTube. Those kids in Seattle. They robbed a seafood store and tossed these big fish back and forth. It was a riot. The store owners were hiding behind their table, and the fish were flying every-where."

"Yeah, and it got them, like, half a million hits," Jack said. "Everyone in Seattle knows who they are."

"And they didn't get in any trouble?" Ivy asked.

"No way," Jack told her. "It was just a funny video. You know. A total fake. The owner of the seafood store was in on it."

"And I guess it got the store a load of publicity," I said.

"Yeah. Everyone liked it," Jack replied. "We can do the same thing. Everyone in Shadyside will know us. Ha. The Shadyside Shade."

Ivy's face was locked in a frown. I could see she still wasn't buying the idea. And I didn't blame her. She was the one who came out of our last prank with a blown-up car. She was the one who'd had her summer in New York ruined because of it.

"Listen, guys," she said, her eyes on me. "How about we come up with something less dangerous?"

Jack sighed. He swept a hand back over his spiky white-blond hair. "It won't be dangerous, Ivy. Everyone will be in on it. The store owner will be playing along, too. What could be dangerous?"

Ivy thought for a moment. "What if someone wanders into the store who isn't in on the joke?"

"We'll make sure that doesn't happen," Jack said. "We can always stop the live stream video and explain. Right?"

A hush fell over the room. Everyone was thinking about the prank, trying to picture it. Finally, I broke the silence. "I think we should do it," I said. "I mean, we've been under a lot of stress. All these tests are killing me . . . All the pressure at school . . . Who is going to blame us for blowing off some steam?"

I thought I had to be enthusiastic about the plan. After all, I wanted to impress Jack. I had a major-league crush on him, and I wanted him to like me back.

So I got all rah-rah about the robbery plan. And my enthusiasm can be infectious. It's one of my best qualities, I think. And after a little more discussion, even Ivy was willing to participate.

"Let's all get famous!" I cheered.

Jeremy narrowed his eyes at Jack. "Have you thought of a store? What kind of store are we going to pretend to rob?"

"How about a Burger King?" Manny chimed in. "I'm getting hungry."

"I've been thinking about it," Jack said. His silvery eyes flashed.

"That would be funny, right?" Manny continued. "If we robbed a big bunch of Whoppers and fries? We could be the Flame-Broiling Robbers. Let's say we stole a hundred Whoppers. That could maybe get us in *Guinness World Records*. The first ones in history to steal a hundred Whoppers? How awesome is that?"

Jack kept a hard stare on Manny, who was practically hopping up and down in his chair, he was so excited. Finally, Jack said, "Are you finished?"

I laughed. "Manny, I can't tell if you're serious or not! But you're making *me* hungry, too."

Manny's face stretched into the dopey grin that was his natural expression. He laughed. "I'm always serious."

"Seriously deranged," Ivy said. She reached out a hand and messed up his hair.

Manny made two fists and pretended he was going to sock her.

I could see that Jack was getting impatient. "So? Do you have a store in mind?" I asked.

He nodded. "Harlow's."

I blinked. "Harlow's Pic 'n' Pay? Here on River Road? Why Harlow's?"

"A lot of reasons," Jack said. "One, it's never crowded. It's kind of out of the way. Two, it's small, with narrow aisles, and the cash register is right near the front door. And three, Harlow is a really nice guy. He's even nice to teenagers."

Manny laughed. "Why would anyone be nice to teenagers?"

"He's a good dude. He'll go along with a joke," Jack said. He clapped his hands together. "Everyone raise your right hand. Like taking an oath. We're going to do this thing and it's going to be awesome, and we're all going to be famous."

We all raised a hand high. Manny raised both hands. Ivy was the last to do it. I could see she still had her doubts.

After Jeremy, Ivy, and Manny had left, I found myself on Jack's lap, his arms wrapped tightly around me. He ran a hand over my springy hair. I think he liked the way it bounced. We nuzzled our faces for a little while, just teasing each other, and then we kissed, a long, hard kiss that took my breath away.

"You're amazing," he growled, soft and low.

With our second kiss, he wrapped me up even tighter. The back of my neck tingled and I felt chills run down my spine. His lips were hard, not soft. I didn't know what that meant. I couldn't think clearly. Actually, I couldn't think at all.

But as I pressed my hands on his cheeks and kissed him, I found myself thinking about our store robbery. Just another prank by the Shadyside Shade.

I was right to go along with the idea.

Because this—what I was feeling with Jack—couldn't be wrong.

21

POPPY CONTINUES

A few nights later, Jack, Ivy, and I drove to Harlow's to check out the store and plan some things. Jeremy couldn't come with us. He'd had an asthma attack during sixth period at school, a pretty bad one, I guess, because an ambulance came for him and took him away.

Ivy texted him around dinnertime. He said he was home but still feeling weird and not breathing normally.

And Manny . . . we couldn't find him. He didn't answer his phone. We had no idea where he was.

A wide asphalt driveway leads up to Harlow's, which sits on a low hill overlooking River Road. The front of the store is all glass, a big window. There's no window display, except for a few neon beer signs. You can see the aisles inside the brightly lit store. A red neon sign above the glass entrance reads: *Pic 'n' Pay. No checks accepted.*

Ivy and I followed Jack in. Mr. Harlow was leaning over the front counter, reading a newspaper. He glanced up as we entered and nodded hello. He's pretty old, maybe in his fifties or sixties. He has silvery hair, tanned cheeks with lots of little crisscross lines in them, and dark eyes that only half open, like he's always drowsy or something.

It was a warm spring night, but Harlow was wearing a checked flannel shirt, red and black like a lumberjack shirt. Everything else he was wearing was hidden behind the counter. "Let me know if I can help you," he said. He has a warm, friendly voice, with just a touch of a southern accent.

We made our way to the long beer display refrigerator that runs the whole length of the back wall. A small black radio on the shelf behind the front counter was playing a baseball game. Harlow had his head down, studying his newspaper.

"I see two security cameras," Jack said in a low voice. He motioned with his head. "One above the back wall, one over the front counter."

Ivy and I followed Jack's gaze. "Don't all look at

once," he scolded. "Do you really want to look like you're casing the joint?"

"You're right," I murmured. "We've got to be subtle."

We moved farther along the beer display. A chill came off the glass. A gray cat watched from an aisle opposite us.

My heart was pounding. No reason to be nervous. We were just checking things out. Jack tapped my shoulder. "See the back door? It leads to a small parking lot. We can park back there, avoid the bright lights up front."

"Do you believe this?" Ivy called loudly. She held up a package. "Carrot Cake Oreos? Are they *kidding*?"

"They make a lot of flavors now," Harlow said, raising his head from his newspaper. "No one likes them."

Something happened in the baseball game. The sounds of the crowd cheering rang from the radio. Harlow shook his head unhappily. "The O's just blew another one." He slammed his newspaper shut. "You guys ever been to Camden Yards? It's a nifty little park." He sighed. "Deserves better than this."

"My dad is a baseball fan," Ivy told him, replacing the Oreos on the shelf. "But he roots for the Pirates."

"National League." Harlow said the words as if they were curse words. "They make the pitchers bat." He turned to Ivy. "Where'd your dad grow up?"

"Franklin Park," she said. "I was born there, but we moved to Shadyside when I was four."

As they talked, I moved toward the back of the store. I passed the long display racks of chips and salsa, and I thought, *Why don't we just tear open a few bags of chips, pull out some beers, and have a nice friendly talk with the guy we're going to rob in a few days?*

Of course, the whole thing wasn't that weird since Jack planned to let Harlow in on it and rehearse the whole thing with him.

"We need to get Manny here," Jack whispered to me, his eyes on the headlights rolling up in the front parking lot. "He needs to get an idea of the layout since he'll be the video guy."

"I'll try him again," I said, pulling out my phone.

A young couple entered the store, greeted Harlow, and made their way to the coffee machine.

I spotted a narrow door in the back wall and walked over to investigate it. I found myself in a small back room. A single fluorescent ceiling bulb cast gray light down over shelves of what looked to be cleaning supplies. An old soda dispenser lay on its side on the floor. Four large metal trash cans lined one wall.

Nothing interesting back here, I thought. I was so busy studying the cluttered shelves in the gray light that I didn't see the tall, skinny guy in the middle of the room until he called out. "Hey."

Startled, I gasped.

He leaned on the handle of a wide push-broom. He wore a sleeveless black T-shirt and very baggy jeans. He had dark, scraggly hair, a mass of it falling over one eye. His silver nose ring gleamed under the fluorescent light.

It took me a few seconds to catch my breath. He stared at me, both hands wrapped around the broom handle, and didn't say a word. He had funny eyes. They didn't stay still. They kind of danced around.

"I . . . I'm sorry," I stammered. "I didn't see you."

He didn't reply. Just brushed the wave of hair off his eye.

"I thought this was the bathroom," I lied.

Why didn't he say anything? He was seriously creeping me out.

"Do you work for Mr. Harlow?" I asked. I backed up toward the door.

He nodded. "My name is Lucas," he said finally.

"Oh. Hi. Hi, Lucas."

He stared at me, leaning on the broom, the strange

eyes doing somersaults in his head. He appeared to be about my age, but I'd never seen him at school.

"Well . . . sorry," I said. "Hope I didn't startle you." I backed up a few more steps.

And the door slammed shut behind me.

I gasped and spun around.

I'm shut up in this room with this creep.

He leaned the broom handle against a shelf and took a step toward me. His crazy eyes were locked on me. I felt . . . invaded. Like he was trying to see more than he should.

"The door—" I started.

He moved closer.

I could feel cold panic rising up inside me, freezing me in place. "The door—"

He moved quickly. A few inches from me now. And then he stepped past me and made his way with long strides to the door.

He shoved the door open. "It does that sometimes," he said. His smile revealed crooked teeth. "Don't know why. Maybe it's haunted. Ha."

"Scared me," I said. I forced a laugh. "I think I jumped a mile."

He nodded but didn't reply.

I was starting to feel more normal. I stepped past him, back into the store. "Bye, Lucas. Sorry to interrupt you."

I could feel his eyes on me as I walked away. He called after me, "No problem, Poppy."

I hurried to catch up to my friends. Ivy and Jack were waving good-bye to Harlow. I still felt tense. Something about that guy gave off very bad vibes.

Yes, I'd overreacted when the door slammed. But I still didn't feel safe.

I was out in the parking lot, about to climb into Jack's borrowed SUV, when the question finally dawned on me: *Whoa, wait. Lucas . . . He called me Poppy. How did he know my name?*

22

POPPY CONTINUES

When I'm on the treadmill, I like to start at a slow, uphill walk, then go faster every five minutes or so, until I'm doing a good run—nothing impressive, but a nice steady trot. I do the treadmill and then the stationary bike for twenty minutes or so. I get my muscles warmed up and my heart pumping, and that's all the cardio I need.

A lot of kids were skeptical when they added on a full exercise gym to our high school. And I know a lot of parents were angry because they didn't want to pay for it. But I think everyone was surprised by how many kids want to use it. After most school days, the place is rocking.

Today, there was no Drama Club meeting after school

because Mr. G is still rehearsing everyone in *Don't Go There!*, his play. Since the play couldn't go on as scheduled because of an "unfortunate" car accident, the plan is to present it to the whole school in a week or so.

I didn't want to go home and start my homework or fight with Heather, so I headed to the gym. And I was still in my walking mode on the treadmill when a large, familiar figure climbed onto the machine next to mine.

"Hey, Manny." My voice came out a little breathless, even though I was only walking.

I don't think he saw me. He tapped the controls and began to jog, pumping his hands at his sides.

"Hey, Manny," I called a little louder, and finally he turned to me. He grinned. He was in a Shadyside Tigers training jersey and sweatpants. His big stomach bobbed a little as he trotted in place.

"Gotta get back in shape," he said. "Wrestling team meeting on Saturday."

I snickered. "When were you ever in shape?"

He laughed, but then he said, "That's cold, Poppy. You know I'm big-boned." He tapped his belly. "This is all rock. Solid muscle."

"If you say so." I grinned at him.

Manny's smile faded. He slowed his treadmill to a

fast walk. "Hey, I saw Keith. Have you seen him?"

"No. We don't have any classes together. Why?"

"He's kind of messed up." Manny studied me, anticipating some kind of reaction. I don't really know what he was expecting. Keith was history. Was I supposed to break down and start producing tears because Manny thought he wasn't in good shape?

"What kind of messed up?" I asked.

Manny scratched his thick, black hair. It was damp, matted to his forehead. He already had a sweat stain on the front of his jersey. "Messed up," he repeated.

"You're so eloquent. Maybe you should try writing poetry, too."

"You still writing poems?"

"Not lately. I've been too busy. But I think about it."

His dark eyes flashed. "Too busy with Jack?"

"Maybe." I reached over and shoved him, knocking him off-balance. "What about Keith?"

"He looks thin and pale. Like he's lost weight."

"Maybe he's on the No-Poppy Diet." I laughed at my own joke. Manny chuckled, too.

"I tried to talk to him," Manny said, "but he just mumbled something I couldn't hear and hurried away." He shook his head. "I don't know what his problem is, but he just didn't look right."

I made a sympathetic sound. I like Keith. Not as a boyfriend. But I like him. I didn't want him to be sick or something.

I realized Manny was staring hard at me. "Keith never did drugs, did he?"

I let out a cry. "Huh? Keith? Straight-arrow Keith? Do drugs? The idea would kill him, Manny. Remember when Ivy's parents were away, and we opened that bottle of red wine?"

"Two bottles," Manny corrected me.

"Who was the only one who didn't get trashed? Remember? Keith refused to drink any wine!"

Manny mopped sweat off his forehead with his arm. "Okay. Okay. Maybe he just has the flu or something." Silence for a while. Then Manny said, "I saw him with that strange guy who dropped out of school last year. Lucas Something-or-Other."

I blinked. "Lucas? I think I met that guy at Harlow's."

Manny nodded. "Yeah, he started working there after he dropped out."

"Why on earth would Keith be hanging with that weirdo?"

Manny shrugged. "Beats me. But I saw them at the

elementary school playground. Keith was picking up his little brother, and Lucas was with him."

"No way," I said, shaking my head. "No way. You know what you need? You need to have your eyes examined. Keith would never hang out with someone like that. Someone who dropped out of school? Who sweeps up in a convenience store? Someone with a *nose ring*? That's not quite Keith's style."

Manny shrugged. "I saw what I saw."

"I'll ask my sister where she buys her eyeglasses," I said. That seemed to end the conversation about Keith.

I picked my speed up a few notches. I forced myself to think about other things. I didn't want to think about Keith. I didn't really care who he was hanging out with.

A few minutes went by, then I asked, "Don't you want to hear how the robbery plans are going?"

He glanced around, I guess to see if anyone could overhear us. "How are the robbery plans going?"

"It's going to be awesome. We went to Harlow's store." I squinted at him. "Where were you, by the way? I kept calling."

He tossed his hands up. "Home. My phone went dead and I didn't know it. No one could reach me. I thought maybe I wasn't popular anymore."

"You're not," I joked.

His big shoes pounded the treadmill. "So you went to the store? And?"

"Harlow is going to cooperate totally. He didn't get the idea at first. He thought we were really going to rob him. But Jack explained it really well, how it was just an internet hoax, and he told him how many thousands of views we'll probably get."

"And what did Harlow say?"

"He said he could use the publicity. He's kind of isolated up there on River Road. Doesn't get that much traffic. Then he told some long, boring story about how they held Senior Prank Week when he went to Shadyside and how much fun it was until something or other happened and the administration banned it. Anyway, he was fine with it." I pumped my fist in the air. "We're good to go."

Manny grinned. "Cool."

"Did Jack talk to you about visiting the store? Checking out the best place for you to record the robbery?"

Manny nodded. The front of his shirt was drenched in sweat now. His big legs churned as he thudded the treadmill. "I already went there. I think the best thing is for me to go in with you guys on the night of the robbery.

You know. Follow from behind. Then I can stay in the front of the store and focus back and forth on Harlow and then you all."

"Sounds good," I said. "Jack thinks we should do the thing on a weekday night. You know. So the store isn't too crowded."

Manny's eyes flashed. "But I might have homework."

I laughed. "Funny guy." I could feel the muscles in my thighs now. I was getting a good workout. "It's going to go viral," I said. "It's going to be huge."

"I know that's why you and Ivy agreed to do it," he said. "You both want to be stars." He slowed his machine and tapped me on the shoulder. "I have only one problem," he said softly. "My brother."

"Benny?"

He nodded. "Yeah. Benny is a cop, remember."

"How could I forget?"

"Well . . . don't you think someone should tell him what we're going to do? I mean, if it's just a joke, shouldn't we let the police know . . . just in case?"

"Just in case what?"

"In case someone calls it in to them. Another customer at Harlow's. Or someone sees us from the parking lot and calls 911. Shouldn't I at least tell Benny what's going down?"

I worried about it for a few moments. What would Jack say?

"I don't think you should tell Benny. It's just a joke. It will be over in two minutes. Why get the police involved?"

Walking to my car in the student parking lot, my legs ached, but it was a good kind of ache. It was a cloudy afternoon but warm, threatening a spring rain. In Shadyside Park behind the high school, tall spring flowers were bending and swaying in the swirls of wind.

The lot was nearly deserted. It was after four and most kids had already left. I stopped when I saw a flash of black near the end of the lot. Was someone there?

The wind blew my hair back. The trees in the schoolyard appeared to shiver, shaking their newly sprouted leaves. I saw something move along the side of a blue SUV.

Yes. A person. Someone was definitely there. It was hard to see in the deepening gray light. Someone moving quickly. I saw a blur of motion to the wide tree near the building at the side of the lot.

"Hello?" I called. I'm not sure why. I guess because whoever it was was trying not to be seen.

No answer to my call.

But I knew someone was hiding behind the tree.

Hiding behind the tree and watching me?

"Is someone there?" My voice was muffled by a strong gust of wind.

No reply.

I know you're there.

A shiver ran down my back. I felt a cold drop of rain on my forehead. I ran to my car, pulled open the door, and slid inside. I started the engine, then quickly locked the doors.

My eyes were on the tree by the school. I couldn't see anyone. No sign of anything. But I knew someone was hiding there. I'm not crazy and I have 20/20 vision.

My mind spun with questions. *Was it Keith? Was he so upset I broke up with him that he's stalking me?*

Crazy thoughts. *That's not like Keith at all.*

I tore out of the spot, leaving whoever it was in my rearview mirror.

There was an accident on River Road and traffic crawled along. I passed Harlow's Pic 'n' Pay on the way up to my home. There were three or four cars in the parking lot.

I thought about our planned prank. How could we make sure there were no customers when we burst in to rob the place? Had I given Manny the right advice when

I told him not to tell his brother about it?

I had to talk to Jack. So many questions.

I didn't get home till after five, and I knew Mom would be angry. I'd promised to help with dinner, and—oh no! I'd promised to pick up the chicken breasts at the market on my way home—and I completely forgot.

Oh, wow.

"Hey, Mom—are you home?" I darted through the back hall to the kitchen. "Mom—I forgot the chicken."

Heather stepped into the hall. She had a stack of potato chips in her hand. Her hair was unbrushed, and she had a smear of food on one cheek. "Mom isn't home yet. She had some kind of emergency with her bees at the lab."

"They're hornets." I wiped the stain off Heather's cheek with one finger. "What's going on? Is it snack time?"

"No." She shoved a few chips into her mouth and chewed for a while. "I'm not staying for dinner."

"You're going out?"

She nodded. "Rose and I are going to see *Romeo and Juliet* at the Town Center. Then she says she's going to rehearse me. You know. Train me in Juliet's part."

I couldn't help myself. I laughed.

Heather's features instantly tightened in anger. "What's so funny?"

I should have shut up. Her quick anger was a clue to rein myself in. But, for some reason, I couldn't do it.

"Do you really think Rose *likes* you?" I blurted out. "Don't you think she's using you? Just trying to make me angry?"

I regretted the words as soon as I'd said them.

Heather's face darkened to a deep red, and her chin trembled. She balled her hands into fists. Her body shuddered, like a volcano preparing to go off.

Had I really said that? I'd only meant to think it. I hadn't meant to say it out loud.

She made a sputtering sound, and I thought she was about to explode on me. But no. She spun around hard, her fists whirling at her sides, and stormed toward the front door.

"Heather, wait—" I called, lurching after her. "Heather—please. I . . . I'm sorry. I—"

The door slammed in my face.

23

POPPY CONTINUES THE STORY

The night of the robbery, a Thursday night, we met at Jeremy's house since his parents were at a meeting across town. Jeremy pulled some cans of beer from the fridge in his basement game room. He said his parents would never notice.

He and Manny snapped open cans and clinked them together as if toasting. Ivy and I decided no. I think we were both too jumpy.

"I want to stay alert," I said. "You know how I get after one beer."

"No, we don't," Manny said with that grin that is his natural expression. "Show us."

"Shut up," Ivy said. "We have to stay sharp, don't

we? It's not like we rob a store every night."

Jeremy's parents have an air-hockey table, a foosball table, and a couple of vintage pinball machines. And they have an actual bar—red vinyl—with rows of sparkly, dark bottles lined up in front of a fancy mirror, and tall stools we used to climb onto when we were younger and pretend to order drinks.

We used to hang out down here all the time when we were kids. We thought it was the coolest place on earth. Now, we were all leaning against the air-hockey table, but none of us was tempted to play.

Manny and Jeremy clinked cans again. Manny had a foam mustache already. He really is a slob.

I felt jittery. My skin tingled. My mouth felt dry as cotton. Maybe I *did* need a beer.

Ivy kept playing with her hair, tying it behind her head, then letting it go. "Hey, we both wore the same outfit," she said, eyeing me. Black skirt and tights, dark-blue long-sleeved top.

"It's my robbery outfit," I said.

"It'll look good in the video," Manny said, checking his phone for the hundredth time. "All powered up."

"Where is Jack?" Jeremy demanded. "He's late."

"He said he had to pick some things up," I said.

Manny took a long gulp of beer and then burped.

"Fourth-grader," I murmured.

He grinned. "And proud of it."

"I don't like this standing around," Ivy said. "It's making me really tense."

"Why should we feel tense? Just because we're robbing a store?" I joked.

"We're taking two cars, right?" Manny said, spinning his beer can on the air-hockey table. "Mine and Jack's?"

"That's what he said," I answered. "I think—"

I stopped when I heard heavy footsteps thudding down the basement stairs.

We all turned to the stairway.

"Everybody freeze!" a voice boomed. "Shadyside Police!"

I gasped. I saw Ivy grip the side of the table.

Jack came bursting into the room, grinning, a cardboard box in his arms.

"You're not funny!" Ivy cried. "You really scared me."

Jack snickered. "You're too easy."

"Well, we're all tense," I said.

He set the carton on the air-hockey table. "No need to

be tense. It's going to be cake. A piece of cake." He gazed around the table, taking attendance. "Okay. Good. Hey, you got a beer for me?"

Jeremy started to the half fridge beside the bar. But Jack stepped in his way and stopped him. "No. Wait. Better save the beer for celebrating afterward."

Manny glugged down the rest of his beer and crushed the can in his hand. "I like to celebrate before *and* after."

Jack tugged down the sleeves of his black Nirvana sweatshirt. His eyes flashed, silvery under the basement ceiling lights. His smile faded and his expression turned hard, all business.

He pulled the carton closer and reached inside. "Here. Everyone take one." He pulled out a handful of black ski masks.

I felt a chill at the back of my neck. This was getting real.

Of course, it *wasn't* real. Jack had assured us a hundred times that everything was taken care of, that everything was cool with Mr. Harlow, that nothing real or dangerous could interrupt our little fantasy robbery.

But something about the ski masks, maybe the solemn black color, sent a chill, and made my whole body feel tingly and my mind more alert.

Jeremy took a mask from Jack and examined it. "Is

this a synthetic fabric or is it wool?" he asked, turning the mask in his hands, searching for a label. "I'm allergic to wool."

Jack let out an exasperated groan. "It's not wool, Jeremy. It's fake. But so what? You only need to wear it for five minutes."

Jeremy studied the ski mask unhappily. "Are you sure?"

"Do we have to wear them?" Ivy asked. I knew she was probably worried about messing up her hair. "I mean, we want everyone to recognize us, right? We want everyone watching online to know it's us."

Jack groaned again and tossed a mask at her. It bounced off her shoulder. "You can't hold up a store without wearing a mask," he said, unable to hide his impatience. "Have you ever heard of anyone robbing a store and showing their face to the security cameras? Have you?"

Ivy blushed. "Guess not."

"No one could be that stupid," Jack snapped.

"I'm not stupid!" Ivy cried, slapping the mask against the tabletop.

"Let's all chill," Jeremy said. "We're stressed out and—"

"No reason to be stressed out," Jack said. His eyes

flashed. "We're doing this for a laugh, remember?"

Jeremy shrugged. "It doesn't feel like it."

"Lighten up, guys," Jack said. "We drive to the store. We're in, we're out. And we have to make it look as real as we can." He turned to Manny. "You checked your phone?"

Manny nodded. "Checked and double checked. No worries."

I ran the mask through my hands. The material felt scratchy and rough. I realized my hands were ice cold. *Jack is right. This is supposed to be fun,* I scolded myself. *Just think about the awesome reaction we're going to get when we pull this stunt off.*

"Focus, everyone," Jack said. "When we go online, keep it serious, okay? Keep it real. And listen . . ."

"We're listening," Ivy muttered, rolling her eyes.

Jack ignored her. "When we're online, don't anyone use real names. Just stick to the names we rehearsed, okay?"

Yes. We'd gone over this before. It was my idea. "This is like play-acting," I told everyone. "We each pick a role to play." I thought everyone would enjoy it more if they felt like they were actors playing a part.

I was Robin. Jack was Trevor. Robin and Trevor.

Ivy was Diana. Jeremy was Thomas. And Manny . . . I couldn't remember Manny's character name. It didn't matter. He wouldn't be on-camera anyway.

I watched Jack as he continued his last-minute instructions. He certainly was thorough. All business. I figured that was a good thing. No slipups. No surprises.

Boy, was I wrong.

24

POPPY CONTINUES

"Are we ready?" I asked. I could feel the blood pulsing at my ears. I knew I was excited. Excited and just a little afraid.

Jack drew close and squeezed my arm gently. "It's going to be *awesome*," he whispered in my ear.

Then he turned back to the others. "Okay. Keep it real, everyone. And don't hold back. It's a robbery, remember. Harlow will play along. He's ready. He's going to be great."

Jeremy tossed his beer can in the wastebasket behind the bar. Ivy and I started to the basement stairs.

"Oh, wait. One more thing," Jack said. He motioned us back to the air-hockey table.

I groaned. I was eager to get the show on the road. Too much time in Jeremy's basement was making me tenser and tenser. I felt like a rubber band all twisted tight. I wanted to spin free.

We all gathered at the table again. Manny had his phone raised and appeared to be texting someone. Jack reached into the carton he had brought—and pulled out a small gray pistol.

"Whoa!" Manny let out a cry and dropped his phone onto the game table.

Ivy and I both gasped. I saw Jeremy narrow his eyes in disbelief, following Jack's hand as he raised the pistol.

Ivy found her voice first. "Jack, come on, dude. You never said we'd bring a gun."

"No way," I protested. "Ivy is right. We've been talking about this for two weeks, and you never said anything about a gun."

Jack scowled at us. "What do you want to rob Harlow with—a popsicle stick?" He twirled the gun in his fingers.

"Is it . . . real?" Jeremy asked timidly, eyes on the twirling pistol.

Jack nodded. "Yeah. It's real."

Shivers started to roll down my back. I wrapped my

arms around myself to stop the trembling.

I have a thing about guns. My dad kept guns in the house. He was kind of a gun nut. He was always taking them out and cleaning them. He kept bullets in a locked drawer in the basement. Sometimes he took a gun to some kind of target practice. I don't know where.

I didn't want to know. I guess I was supposed to feel safe with all those guns around. But I didn't. I was always afraid whenever I saw one. I guess I have too good an imagination. I had all these fantasies of one of us getting shot.

When my parents split and Dad moved out of the house, he took all his guns with him, and I was glad. But now here I was, staring at the gun in Jack's hand, all the bad feelings from my childhood rushing back at me.

"Let's roll, everyone," Jack said. He took long strides toward the basement steps, waving the pistol like a pennant. "It's showtime."

He glanced back at me. He saw that my eyes were on the gun in his hand. His face grew solemn. "Let's just hope we don't have to use it."

I gave his shoulder a shove. "You're joking—right? Right?"

25

POPPY CONTINUES

Ivy and Jeremy rode with Manny. They followed close behind Jack and me.

Jack didn't have his truck. He was driving a small Mazda two-door. "Where'd you get this car?" I asked, struggling with the seat belt.

"Borrowed it," he murmured, eyes on the road. Headlights washed over our windshield like bright lightning streaks, one after another.

He had the gun beside him between the seats. His mask was in his lap. I turned and saw Manny's headlights in the rear window. I knew they were as freaked about the gun as I was.

"Hey, Jack," I started. I put my hand on his shoulder.

"We really don't want to do this. Not with a . . . a weapon."

He brushed my hand away gently. "It's loaded with blanks, Poppy."

Traffic slowed as River Road curved down toward town. Jack eased his foot on the brake. He was a careful driver. You might expect him to be reckless, wild. It would have fit his personality better. But he didn't drive that way.

"I told you my dad works at the track," he said, wrapping his right hand around the gun handle. "This is the starter pistol he uses at his job."

"No real bullets?" I asked, studying him, trying to make sure he was telling the truth.

"No worries," he said.

He turned sharply into the parking lot at Harlow's. I saw a few cars parked near the front door. The store inside was bright as day. I could see each aisle clearly through the wide front window. I couldn't see the front counter, but I knew Mr. Harlow must be there.

Jack edged the car around the side of the building, and we parked in deep shadow at the far side of the parking lot in back. The back door to the store had a small window in it. But I couldn't see anything in it.

Manny's car slid beside us a few seconds later. He cut his headlights immediately. Jeremy climbed out from the passenger seat. He was breathing heavily, his chest riding up and down. I hoped he wasn't going to have one of his asthma attacks.

Ivy stepped out from the back seat and took Jeremy's arm. "It's a warm night, but I'm shivering," she whispered.

The five of us huddled together in the shadows behind our cars. Manny waved his phone in front of him. "Ready to go live?"

"Not yet." Jack grabbed Manny's hand and pushed it down. "We have to make sure no one else is in the store. Just Harlow." He turned to Ivy. "You go."

Ivy started toward the back door. Jack hurried after her. "No. Go in the front. Act like a customer. See what's going on."

Manny grinned. "It's called casing the joint."

Jack frowned at him. "Think you could be a little more serious?"

Manny shrugged. "Don't any of you watch movies?"

I heard a car horn from the front of the store. Car doors slammed. I heard the car pull away.

Clouds covered the half-moon and the air grew

cooler. A gust of wind made my hair fly up, and I struggled to smooth it down with both hands.

"What's keeping Ivy?" Jeremy asked, his voice strained. He kept crossing and uncrossing his arms.

"She probably got a hero or something," Manny said. "I don't think she had dinner."

"She's waiting for the store to be empty," Jack said. "Don't worry. When it's showtime, she'll give us a signal."

I could feel drops of sweat on my forehead. My legs felt jumpy. I wanted to get going. Get this stunt over with. I kept fiddling with the scarf around my neck, twisting it one way then the other.

Finally, Ivy reappeared, walking rapidly along the side of the store. She didn't signal or anything. She waited until she was back in the safety of the shadows behind our cars.

"There were some kids from school buying slushies," she said breathlessly. "But they left."

"So who's in there now?" Jack demanded. "Just Harlow?"

"Yeah. Harlow," Ivy answered. "And that weird guy, Lucas, who sweeps up."

"He won't be a problem," Jack said. "He's like a

zombie or something." He turned to us. "Ready to rumble?"

We all muttered yes. Manny started punching his phone. "Ready for the live stream. This is going to be awesome!"

We started toward the back door but Jack jumped ahead and stopped us. "Aren't you forgetting something? Like ski masks?"

We'd left them in the cars. It took a short while to find them and pull them on.

"Let's go in the front," Jack said. "Much better light."

Manny had his mask on and his phone raised. "I won't push *record* till we go in."

"Remember—let's go in *loud*!" Jack said. "We want to make it look like we've scared Harlow to death— right? So let's go in screaming."

We edged our way along the side of the building. I could feel my heart start to flutter in my chest as we stepped into the light from the front window.

Manny tugged open the door and went in first. I knew he wanted to get in a good position to capture the whole thing.

Jeremy and Ivy followed. As I started through the doorway, I felt something hard in my hand. It took a second or two to realize that Jack had slid the pistol into my hand.

I nearly dropped it. My fingers wrapped themselves tightly around the handle.

"Go!" Jack whispered.

And we burst toward the front counter, all of us screaming at the top of our lungs. *"This is a robbery!"*

26

POPPY NARRATES

My mask slipped and the eye holes moved. I couldn't see a thing. I stumbled and bumped into Ivy and nearly knocked her over. Jack grabbed my shoulder and steadied me.

"Hands high! This is a robbery!" Jack screamed.

Manny leaped to the side of the counter and trained his phone lens on us. I pulled at the mask with my free hand until I could see again.

Harlow had been leaning on the counter, hair down over his forehead, typing on an iPad. As we burst forward, screaming, his eyes went wide, his arms flew up, and he backed up till he hit the cigarette display on the wall. A frightened squeak escaped his lips.

My brain was doing flip-flops. *Jack said Harlow was in on the joke*, I thought. *He looks really frightened.*

Out of the corner of my eye, I glimpsed that weird guy, Lucas. He was leaning on a broom by the door to the little supply room. His dark eyes were wide and his mouth hung open, but he didn't move. He stood there like a statue, one hand on the broom handle, one hand suspended in air as if he was the one being robbed.

"Pull out all your cash. Hurry!" Jack ordered. His voice was muffled by the black mask. "Hurry!"

Harlow squinted hard and eyed him as if trying to identify him. He took a step toward the counter, but he didn't make a move to open his cash drawer.

"You kids don't want to do this," he said quietly. He glanced from Jeremy to Ivy to me. "Trust me. You want to leave now and think later about how you *almost* ruined your lives."

"Shut up!" Jack screamed. He sounded so angry he made me jump. I felt my heart leap into my throat.

"Listen to me," Harlow insisted, returning Jack's stare. "This isn't worth it. You're going to be caught. Your lives—all of you—will be wrecked."

What is happening? I wondered. *He's supposed to be in on the joke!*

I was there when Jack spoke to him. He was in on it. Was he just a good actor?

"If you turn around and leave now, I won't call the police or make any complaint," Harlow continued. He tapped the counter with his fingertips, the only sign he might be nervous. "Do you hear me?"

"Shut up!" Jack screamed again. "Shut up, shut up, shut up! I'm warning you, old man."

He and Harlow continued their staring match.

"Just hand over the cash," Jack ordered. "Hand it over—no more crap!"

Harlow nodded. His expression changed. He tightened his lips and his eyes grew cold.

"Hurry!" Jack screamed.

Harlow reached for the drawer in the counter and began to pull it open.

Jack bumped my shoulder hard. I cried out, startled.

"He's going for his gun," Jack shouted. "Shoot him! Shoot him—fast—Poppy!"

I raised the pistol. I couldn't think. Everything went bright white, as if there was some kind of electrical surge. I felt a surge in my brain, too. As if a powerful charge was burning away all thought.

"Shoot him!" Jack cried.

And the gun went off. I didn't even mean to pull the trigger. The gun went off with a powerful explosion, powerful enough to make my arm jerk behind me. So loud. So loud.

The gun went off—and Harlow grabbed his head with both hands.

I shot him in the head!

A long horrifying groan of pain escaped Harlow's open mouth. His eyes rolled up in his head. His hands fell away from his face, and he slumped behind the counter, hitting the floor with a heavy thud.

"Nooooooo!" I shrieked. "Noooooo! I shot him. I shot him."

I spun away, the floor tilting and swaying. I waved frantically at Manny. "Turn it off! Turn it off, Manny. I shot him. I shot him in the head!"

27

POPPY CONTINUES

My legs were shaking like rubber. My knees started to fold. I was still gripping the gun. It felt as if it weighed a hundred pounds in my hand.

Manny didn't move. He kept his lens locked on us.

"P-please . . . ," I stuttered. "I . . . shot . . . him."

Ivy and Jeremy stared at me. Even through the masks I could see the horror in their eyes.

I gasped as Jack burst out laughing.

He pumped both fists in the air. "That was awesome!" he cried. He turned to Manny. "Did you stop it? Is the live stream off? Any way to know how many people were watching?"

Manny didn't reply. He kept the phone aimed in front of him.

Jack spun around and threw his arms around me. He pressed me in a tight hug. Our ski masks slid together in a scratchy embrace.

"Poppy, you were great! Great!" Jack cried. "I believed it. Everyone will believe it. Poppy, you made it so real!"

I was too stunned to speak. I wanted Jack to hold on to me. I needed his arms around me to stop the trembling. I wanted his face pressed against mine, even through the masks.

But he quickly turned away. "Okay, Mr. Harlow," he called. "The video is over. You can get up now."

We all stared at the front counter.

"You were great," Jack called to him. "Thanks for playing along with us."

Silence. No reply. And no movement behind the counter.

I sucked in a deep breath and held it. We all watched as if we were frozen, stared at the counter, at the cigarette display behind it, at the red Coca-Cola sign at one side.

"Mr. Harlow? Are you okay?" Ivy was the one to call out. She took a cautious step toward the counter.

But Jack dodged around her and stepped behind the counter. He dropped to his knees.

I realized I was still holding my breath. "What is happening?" The words slipped from my mouth. "Jack—tell us!"

And then Jack's voice rose from down on the floor, high and shrill. "Oh nooooo. No! No!"

"Jack? What's wrong?" I choked out.

"He's dead. You *really* shot him, Poppy."

"But, Jack—"

I screamed when I saw the dark-red puddle spread out on the floor from under the counter.

"I thought it was loaded with blanks," Jack said, still down on the floor, hidden behind the counter. "I really did. But he's dead. You killed him."

Silence. And then Jack's shrill cry—

"Everyone, run. Run. Let's get out of here!"

PART TWO

28

POPPY CONTINUES THE STORY

"What do we do now?"

"We can't just drive home and pretend we're okay."

"But where can we go?"

"How many people watched the whole thing online? They must all be calling the police."

We were speeding away in Manny's car. Ivy and Jeremy in the back seat. I was hunched in the front beside Manny, hugging myself, trying to stop the racking shudders that ran down my whole body.

I felt sick. I struggled to keep from throwing up as Manny sped along River Road.

I killed a man. I killed him. I saw his blood pooling on the linoleum floor.

"Where are we going?" Ivy cried.

"Away," Manny said.

"Why did Jack stay?" Jeremy cried, his voice revealing his fear. "Why didn't he run like we did?"

"Who knows?" Manny replied. He slowed at a stoplight. He raised his phone. I couldn't believe he still had it gripped in his hand.

"Ohmigod," he murmured. "I messed up. I never turned off the live stream. The whole thing went online."

A wave of nausea rolled over me. I felt my dinner rise up to my throat. I choked it back down. "But . . . when Jack said Harlow was dead, he used my name. *My real name*." My head was spinning. I tightened my throat and battled my nausea.

"You all heard him," I continued. "You all heard him say, 'You really shot him, Poppy.' And everyone else heard it, too."

Ivy leaned forward from the back seat and patted my shoulder. "That doesn't mean—" she started.

I pushed her hand away. "How many Poppys do you know?" I screamed. I was losing it, but I couldn't help myself. "How many Poppys are there in Shadyside? How many have this stupid name?"

"Poppy, you're screaming," Jeremy said. "Take a breath. Try—"

"My life is over!" I wailed. "Don't you understand? My life is done. Finished. 'Poppy, you killed him.' How many people heard that? And there it is. It's still online, right? Everyone will know I'm a murderer. I killed that nice man. Everyone will know. Everyone. I—I—"

I started to gag. I couldn't keep it down any longer. "Manny," I groaned. "Pull over."

He slowed the car and edged onto the grassy shoulder. I shoved open the passenger door, leaned out, and vomited. I couldn't stop it. It just came spewing up, and I made horrible groaning, grunting sounds as wave after wave poured from my mouth.

When I was finished, I leaned back into the car, pressed my back against the seat, swallowing hard and waiting for the shudders to stop. Manny pulled some paper towels from the glove compartment, and I wiped off my mouth. He edged the car back onto the road.

"Poppy, we can explain this whole thing," Ivy said.

"Huh?" I gasped. "Explain? How?"

"It's not your fault. It's Jack's," Ivy said. "He gave you the gun. He said it wasn't loaded. He told you to shoot."

"But I did it!" I screamed, making my raw throat ache. "I did it, Ivy. I killed Harlow. It was supposed to be a joke. He was a good sport, and now he's dead. I killed him, and the police will never believe it was an accident."

"We can talk to my brother," Manny said, honking at a driver who turned without signaling. "Benny will believe us. He'll—"

"Just take me home," I snapped. "I need to think. I have to get myself together. I . . . I'm not ready to talk to anyone. I . . . have to figure it out—"

"We should stick together," Jeremy said. "Not split up. If we all go to the police . . ." His voice trailed off.

"Maybe Jeremy is right," Ivy said. "We can tell the story better—"

"No!" I screamed. "No! No! No!" I grabbed Manny's arm. "My house is right over there. Let me off. I . . . can't deal with this right now."

"Okay, okay." Manny shoved my hand away. "No problem."

A few seconds later, he slowed the car and rolled up my driveway. The lights were off. Mom and Heather weren't home. I felt a wave of relief. *I won't have to tell them right away. I'll have some time to get my head together.*

I pushed open the door and turned to slide out of the car. "I'll call you," I said.

"Yes, we'll keep in touch," Ivy said. She was gripping

Jeremy's hand tightly. "I'm sure Jack will hurry to your house as soon as he can. Let us know what he says."

"Yeah, let us know what you decide to do," Jeremy said. "We'll be waiting."

"You should brush your teeth," Manny said. "Get that sour taste out of your mouth."

I sighed. "Good old Manny. Always so helpful. I *killed* someone and he's worried about my breath."

Manny flinched. I could see I'd hurt him. He was trying to be helpful, I guess. But I didn't care. I didn't care about anything. My life was over.

I stopped at the front door, fumbling for my key in my bag. I expected to hear sirens approaching. I knew it would be easy for the police to figure out where to find their murderer.

Everyone had seen it online. And everyone had heard it.

"Poppy, you killed him."

I shoved open the front door and stumbled into the dark living room. I tossed my bag against the wall. I didn't turn on any lights. I made my way in the dark to the back hall and into the bathroom. I brushed my teeth, thinking about Manny, and drank two glasses of water from the sink tap, and my mouth still felt dry and sour, my throat tight, aching.

I flashed on the ceiling light in my room and dropped heavily onto the edge of the bed. I raised my phone and glanced at the screen. No messages.

Jack, where are you?

Why have you disappeared? I need you here. I need to talk with you. I need . . .

Where was he? And actually, what could he do for me? He couldn't help me or save me.

But I had to talk to him. I wanted him to hold me tight and tell me everything will be all right, even though it wouldn't be. It wouldn't ever be right again.

I needed to talk to him. "Where are you, Jack?" I said out loud, my voice ringing off the walls of the empty house.

I raised the phone to call him. I punched his number with a trembling finger. The phone went right to voice-mail.

"Jack—where *are* you?" I screamed. "Are you on your way here? Pick up! Pick up!"

I stood up and began pacing the length of my room, arms crossed tightly over my chest. I needed to think. I wanted to concentrate on what I would say to the police, how I could describe it so they would know it was an accident, so they would believe me.

But who would believe it?

A robbery that wasn't really a robbery? Just an internet prank?

Who would believe that?

A silly prank with a loaded gun?

How could I ever make anyone believe me?

The whole thing was on video. And it sure looked real. Especially when I shot Mr. Harlow and he went down and didn't come up.

It sure looked real.

I stopped with a sharp cry when I heard the front doorbell chime. And then a hard, pounding knock on the door.

The police. Of course. It hadn't taken them long. Another doorbell chime. So impatient.

They must have seen the lights on in my room. They must know I'm here.

I took a deep breath and strode into the hall. Still holding my breath, I grabbed the front door handle, pushed open the door—and gasped.

29

POPPY CONTINUES

"Mom!" I cried.

"I forgot my house keys," she said. She narrowed her eyes at me. "Did you go out? You don't have any lights on."

"I . . . was in my room." I stepped aside so she could come in.

She flipped on the entryway light, then the living room lights. "Poppy, you went out?"

Yes, I went out, and I killed a man during a fake robbery.

"Yeah. For a little while."

I knew I had to tell my mom what happened. But I wanted to talk to Jack first. I know it was completely irrational, but I still clung to the idea that Jack could help me.

Mom dropped her purse and briefcase on a chair. She shook her dark hair out, like a dog shaking itself dry. "Whew. I'm toast."

I followed her toward the kitchen. "How come you're so late, Mom?"

"We had an emergency at the lab," she said, pulling open the fridge and taking out a bottle of coconut water. She practically lives on coconut water. "Some of the hornets escaped, the ones we were experimenting on today."

I groaned. "Ugh. Don't remind me of those hornets. That day Keith and I visited your lab, we couldn't believe how big they are. It was like a horror movie."

Mom tilted the bottle to her mouth and took a long drink. "Well, today really was like a horror movie," she said when she finished. "Rounding up hornets is a nightmare job. Much harder than just killing them." Mom finished the bottle and began rummaging in the fridge. "I didn't have dinner. Is there anything in the house?"

"I think there's some egg salad," I said. "And maybe some ham."

I can't believe we're talking about egg salad when a few minutes ago, I killed a man.

Where is Jack?

I glanced at my phone. No text. No call.

My mind began to spin again with all kinds of frightening thoughts.

The police were alerted about the live stream. They hurried to the store. Jack was arrested.

Or . . . the police burst in. They shot Jack before he could explain.

Jack was dead because of a stupid joke.

No. Stop it, Poppy. Don't get carried away.

But where was he? Did he think he could run off by himself and get away?

Didn't he care what was happening to me?

I thought hard, picturing everything again. How we pulled on our masks and burst through the front door. And how Jack shoved the gun into my hand. *My* hand. He gave the gun to *me.*

Why?

Why didn't he keep it? Why did he want me to be the one with the gun?

A question I couldn't answer. My brain was filled with questions I couldn't answer. My head suddenly felt as if it weighed a thousand pounds.

I knew I had to tell my mother what I had done.

I couldn't keep it in any longer. I had to let the whole story out.

She was pulling cold cuts and cheese from the fridge, trying to put together a dinner for herself, carrying it to the kitchen counter with the tall stools.

I took a seat at the table with my back to her. I guess I didn't want to look at her when I told the horrible news. I wanted to tell her, but I didn't want to see her face when she heard what I had done.

Where should I start?

"Mom . . . uh . . . I need to tell you something. I'm afraid something very bad has happened." She didn't react, so I continued. "My friends and I, we have sort of a club. We pull off stunts. You know. Pranks. And we put them online so everyone can be in on the joke. We're not the only ones who do it. A lot of people have the same idea. So tonight . . ."

I took a deep shuddering breath. This was harder than I'd thought. But I had no choice. I needed my mother to know. I needed her to understand and to help me.

So I told her everything. The whole night from beginning to horrible end. Once I started talking, it just burst out of me, like a waterfall. It just flowed. I couldn't have stopped even if I'd wanted to. It didn't feel good to tell the story. I kept my eyes on the wall cabinets in front of me. I didn't dare turn around to face her.

But I managed to get the story out. My voice cracked when I described how Mr. Harlow had grabbed his head and fallen to the floor. And by the time I'd finished telling her everything, my mouth was dry and my hands were wet and ice cold.

"It was just a prank," I finished. "It wasn't supposed to hurt anyone. It was a joke, Mom. A joke that went terribly wrong. Jack told me the gun was filled with blanks. That's what he told us all. But it wasn't."

My voice tightened to a harsh whisper. "What do we do, Mom? Please—help me. What do we do now?"

30

POPPY NARRATES

Silence.

It took all my strength to stand up and turn around.

The kitchen was empty. Mom's dinner plate and the stuff from the fridge was on the counter. But she wasn't there.

"Mom?" I called.

I heard clattering at the back door. The door slammed. Mom entered the kitchen, her arms filled with bottles of coconut water. "I went to the garage," she said, setting them on the counter. "We're running low."

I stared at her. "You didn't hear a word I said?"

"Sorry." She carried three bottles to the fridge. "I thought you heard me go out."

I don't have the strength . . . I can't tell the whole story again.

My phone buzzed. I grabbed it off the table. Jack?

No. I read the screen. Manny.

"Hello?" I walked with the phone to the front of the house.

"Poppy, it's me." He sounded frantic.

"Manny, what's happening? Have you heard from Jack? Have you heard anything?"

"No. Listen to me. It's all over the internet. We're all going to be arrested."

I gasped. My hand shook and I almost dropped the phone.

"We have to go to the police," Manny said. "We can't just sit at home and wait."

"Okay," I started, "but—"

"Benny is at the precinct house. You know. The one on Village Road near Parkview?"

"Yeah. Okay." I wasn't really hearing his words. I mean, I was hearing them but they weren't really making sense, as if I was listening to a foreign language.

"Benny will listen to us," Manny said. "He'll understand. I mean, he'll get it."

"But . . . but, Manny," I sputtered. "This is murder.

How understanding will he be?"

"We just have to talk to him," he replied, his voice pulsing in my ear. "He'll treat us okay, Poppy. He's my brother. It was an accident. Totally an accident. I know he'll believe us."

The living room lights were dancing in my head. I struggled to think straight. Was I really about to go to the police station and confess to killing someone?

"Should I bring my mom?" My voice broke as I asked the question. I had the sudden feeling she had followed me. I spun around. She wasn't there.

"No. Just go to the station. Make an excuse and just go. Okay? I already told Benny we were coming."

"But, Manny—"

"Hurry, Poppy. Benny is waiting. You don't have a choice. You have to do this."

I clicked off. My hand gripping the phone was shaking. I felt as if I had a bird batting its wings in my chest.

"Mom, I have to go out!" I shouted down the hall. I didn't want to go back to the kitchen and face her.

"At this time of night?" she called back. "Where are you going?"

"To Ivy's. She forgot the homework. I'll be right back." Amazing how my brain was frozen in panic but I could still come up with a lie.

She shouted something, but I didn't hear her. I scooped the car keys from the bowl in the entryway and dove out the front door, stumbling onto the stoop, grabbing the metal rail to keep myself from falling.

Get it together, Poppy.

But—how?

I stuffed myself behind the wheel, started the car, and began to ease it down River Road. I gritted my jaw to stop from screaming. I kept having the feeling that I might go completely berserk, lose my mind and start wailing and shrieking and pounding my fists against the wheel.

"Whoa!" I cried out. Headlights in my windshield. I'd been driving on the wrong side of the road. I swerved to the right and nearly clipped the mirror off a parked SUV.

A few minutes later, I pulled into the narrow parking lot at the side of the precinct station. All the lights were on in the three-story brick building. But I was surprised to see few cars in the lot. I spotted two black-and-whites parked at the entrance and two or three other cars at the back. But where were my friends' cars?

I switched off the engine and cut the lights. And sat

there staring glassily out the window for a few minutes, not moving, just struggling to breathe normally and to force my heart from fluttering so hard in my chest.

Finally, I took a deep breath, pushed open the car door, and climbed out. The night air felt cool on my burning face. Low clouds covered the moon, but the tall halogen lights over the lot made everything glow nearly as bright as day.

My shoes crunching on the gravel, I made my way toward the entrance, double glass doors with a square of bright yellow light pouring out from inside. A car rolled by on Village Road, window open, hip-hop blasting through the air.

I gripped the door handle, pulled the door open, and stepped inside. Gazing around, I found myself in a waiting room. Wooden chairs and low round tables and a long bench against the wall. The room was empty and, turning, I saw that there was also no one at the high gray metal desk at the back.

I heard voices from the hall behind the desk. And a crackling police radio with a woman's voice reading off numbers. A man's voice shouted, "Where's the coffee?"

I froze a few feet into the room. My eyes swept the chairs and the empty bench again. A folded-up newspaper on a table. Empty coffee cups. A sandwich wrapper.

But where is everyone? I thought.

Where are my friends? What's going on?

How come I'm the only one here?

31

POPPY CONTINUES

"Poppy?"

A deep voice stunned me from my thoughts. I turned to see Benny Kline standing behind the gray desk. His dark eyes were narrowed on me. His pale-blue uniform shirt was tight around his bulging stomach. He had several buttons open, and I could see the black hair that started high on his chest.

"Hi." I cleared my throat and tried again. "Hi, Benny." I raised my eyes to his.

He rubbed his mustache. "I hear you have a story to tell me."

I nodded. "Yeah. Not a happy one."

He motioned with one hand. "Come on back. We'll go to my office."

I followed him into the hall. I gave one last glance behind me, hoping to see Manny or Jeremy and Ivy, Jack. Where was Jack? No sign of anyone.

Benny's "office" was just a cubicle. It had low gray walls and was at the end of a long row of identical spaces. I saw two other officers standing at a long table against the wall, leaning near a coffee machine, and talking in low voices, both gesturing with their hands.

Benny pulled a chair into his cubicle. He had a small desk and a counter along one side of the wall, piled high with papers and files. The light from his computer monitor washed over him as he sat down, as if he was stepping into a spotlight.

"Talk," he said, tapping a pencil on the desktop.

I cleared my throat. I wasn't sure if I could speak or not. I don't think I'd ever been as scared. After all, I was about to confess to a murder. I was about to end my life as I knew it.

"Um . . . I guess maybe I'll begin at the beginning," I started. My hands were clenched together in my lap, so tight they ached. "You see, we formed a sort of club. Just five of us, including Manny. We called ourselves the Shadyside Shade, and the idea was to do pranks. You know. Stunts. And put them online. Just for fun. But . . ."

An image of Mr. Harlow grabbing his head and sinking to the floor flashed into my mind and stopped me from talking. For the hundredth time, I heard the pistol go off, the pistol raised in my hand, and I saw the man collapse behind the counter.

"Poppy?" Benny's voice broke into my horrified thoughts. "Are you okay? Please go on."

Somehow I went on. I managed to tell him the whole story of the robbery.

He set down the pencil he'd been tapping. His dark eyes narrowed on me as I told him about killing Mr. Harlow, narrowed until they were accusing slits. He rubbed his moustache, massaging it, keeping his stare on me.

"I killed him. It was a total accident, Benny. Jack told me the gun wasn't loaded. But it was. It was an accident, I swear. It was my fault, but I . . . I didn't mean . . . I didn't . . ."

The words choked in my throat. I couldn't speak.

He kept massaging his moustache, his face expressionless. "So tell me," he said finally. "You put this online?"

I nodded. "Yes. Manny did."

He lowered his hand to the desktop. He glimpsed his monitor. "If it was online, why haven't I received any phone calls? Why haven't I heard from anyone?"

I blinked. "What do you mean?"

He scratched his chest. "Poppy, if people watch a murder online, don't you think some of them might call the police?"

"I . . . guess." My head was swimming. I really felt as if I was underwater, struggling to pull myself to the surface.

Benny jumped to his feet. "Two of my guys are out sick. Let's go visit the crime scene." He motioned for me to follow him.

I climbed up unsteadily, still feeling as if I was battling ocean waves. "You mean—?"

"Let's check out Harlow's store. See what we can see."

We drove to Harlow's Pic 'n' Pay in silence. The only sound was the droning voice on the police radio. The voice seemed far away. My frightened thoughts completely drowned it out.

The lights were on in the store as we turned into the parking lot. I expected to see patrol cars, but there were none. No sirens. No flashing lights. No yellow crime tape stretched around the building.

Benny pulled the car to the front entrance. He pushed

open his door. "Let's go."

I felt sick. How could something this horrible happen to me? Just because my friends and I were bored? Is that really the reason I ended up killing a man?

Benny waited for me on the sidewalk in front of the store. "Are you okay?"

"Not really," I choked out.

I started toward him. I didn't see any other cars in the lot. Peering into the window, I didn't see anyone in the store.

Benny held the door open and motioned for me to go in first.

My legs were like rubber. My breath was coming in short gasps.

Somehow I managed to walk into the store. Benny followed close behind.

I turned and raised my eyes to the front counter.

And opened my mouth in a shrill scream: "No! I don't believe it!"

32

POPPY NARRATES

Mr. Harlow was leaning on the counter. At my cry, he stood up straight. He grinned at me. "Hey, Poppy. I'm back."

I choked out another cry. "I—I—" I stared at him, speechless.

And when Manny, Ivy, and Jeremy popped up from behind the counter, I thought I was in a dream, a weird, twisted nightmare. They were cheering and laughing, and I couldn't understand what was happening.

I could see they were enjoying my shock.

I glimpsed that weird guy, Lucas, back by the supply room. He had a grin on his face, too. He had his eyes locked on me, and his hungry expression gave me the creeps.

I mean, why was he enjoying this so much?

Benny moved to the counter to join them. Mr. Harlow stepped out. He strode toward me and gave me a hug. "Poppy," he whispered in my ear, "you have some pretty cruel friends."

I began to come down to earth. The floor felt solid again. The lights were still too bright and flashing in my eyes. But I was beginning to think again, to move out of my shock, to realize what was going on.

"You should see the look on your face," Benny said. "You went so pale, we could almost see through your skin."

"Did we really fool you, Poppy?" Manny demanded.

And now I realized everything. Now I knew what they had done. Done to me.

"You—you—" I pointed an accusing finger. I struggled to find the words. "You . . . played a prank on me?"

They nodded, grins stuck on their faces.

Why? Did they hate me so much?

"You . . . you made me think Mr. Harlow was dead. You made me think I was a murderer. For a prank? Why? How could you do this to me?"

"It was Jack," Ivy said. "Jack planned the whole thing."

"Jack?" I cried. "But, why? And why did you go along with him?"

Their smiles faded. Mr. Harlow muttered something I couldn't hear.

"Why?" I screamed, losing control. "Why? Tell me! Why would you let Jack do this to me? Why did you all do this?"

I was screaming at the top of my lungs now. My heart was pumping. I could feel the blood pulse at my temples.

How could they do this to me? I thought they were my friends.

"We never put it online," Manny said. "Don't worry, Poppy. No one saw it. I was just pretending to stream it. That's why no one called the police."

My head spun. It was never online. They kept the joke to themselves.

Jeremy stepped around the counter. He had his phone raised in front of him. "Jack didn't give us much choice," he said. "He can be convincing, you know. Like scary."

"But, Jeremy—"

"Here." He shoved the phone at me. "Take it. Look. Jack wants to talk to you. Maybe he'll explain."

I took the phone from his hand. My brain spun with confusion. Jack was on the phone? Why wasn't he here to enjoy his big prank?

My hand was shaking. I raised the phone close. I saw

Jack on the screen. Jack standing next to Rose Groban.

Rose clung to him, holding his hand, her arm entwined in his. She was leaning on him, her head tilted against his shoulder. She was wearing bright-red lipstick and her mouth was twisted into a cold smile. Her eyes sparkled, even on the phone screen.

"Jack?" I choked out. "Why—?"

"Gotcha back!" Rose exclaimed. "Your car accident ruined my play. But I got you back. Were you scared? Scared you were a murderer?"

She held on to Jack. He didn't say a word. I couldn't read his expression. Did he feel bad at all for me? Did he feel anything?

Jack and Rose. Jack and Rose.

Together.

And suddenly, I remembered her words of warning in the auditorium that day during auditions for the play. She whispered the words in my ear. Such a harsh, angry whisper. She told me to stay away from Jack.

I hadn't gotten it then. I hadn't realized Rose and Jack were a couple.

How stupid was I?

But now I knew. It was Rose and Jack all the time. They had always been together. Of course they had.

They played this awful trick on me.

All of them. All of them did this to me.

And realizing it, I felt myself explode. I just snapped. I could hear a wave rise up and roar in my brain. I could feel the red anger burst up in my chest, anger I'd never felt before.

I felt more than humiliated. I felt betrayed. Betrayed by the only friends I trusted.

With an animal cry, I heaved the phone at Jeremy. He fumbled it in both hands but caught it before it hit the floor.

I tilted back my head. I wanted to roar like a lion, like a beast in a horror movie. I wanted to roar and tear and scratch and attack, attack them all for what they'd done to me.

"Don't you see what you did?" I cried.

They were still huddled behind the front counter. Mr. Harlow moved to the side so he was half-hidden by a Budweiser display. But the others stood and stared as I began to rage.

"I thought I would *die*!" I screamed. "I thought my life was over. How could you think this was a joke? How could you let Jack and Rose do this to me? Put me through such torture?"

I was gasping for breath. But I couldn't stop scream-ing. I couldn't stop the rush of fury bursting from my trembling body. "I thought you were my friends. I trusted you. I didn't do anything to deserve this. How—"

Jeremy raised a hand to stop me. "Poppy, we're sorry. We didn't realize—"

"I *hate* you!" I wailed. "I hate you all!" I sucked in a wheezing breath. I took a few seconds to get myself together. My throat ached from screaming.

They stood there staring at me in horror. Didn't any of them think of how this would destroy me?

Pausing only made my anger stronger. "You picked the *wrong girl* to do this to!" I screamed. "The wrong girl. I'm warning you! I'm warning you now. I'll pay every one of you back!"

I realized I was shaking my fist at them. They actu-ally looked frightened now. "The wrong girl!" I shrieked. "You picked the wrong girl!"

PART THREE

33

POPPY CONTINUES THE STORY

A week went by, and how did I feel? Sad. Lonely without my friends. Still angry. Still ferociously angry. The anger burned in my chest. I couldn't make it cool down.

Every time I saw Ivy in school, she avoided my eyes and her face turned red. I passed Jeremy in the hall several times, and each time he pretended he didn't know me. As if *he* was the injured party. How ridiculous. And Manny . . . Manny kept wanting to talk, but I pushed the big idiot away.

I thought a lot about getting back at all of them, humiliating them in the same way they'd humiliated me. Punishing them for betraying me. Cruel ideas flashed through my mind, but none of them were good enough.

I knew I'd have to calm down before I could think clearly about it. Once my mind was more settled, I knew I could think of the perfect way to get my revenge.

On Wednesday afternoon, I saw Rose and Jack in the student parking lot behind the school. He had her pinned against the side of a car. Their arms were wrapped around each other and they were locked in a long, passionate kiss. I guess they didn't care who watched them. Or maybe they were showing off.

I turned and stomped away in the other direction, my heart bumping and thumping, my hands clamped into tight fists. I knew I couldn't live with this anger for long. I had to do something to force it away. I had to do something.

I spent a lonely weekend. At least having no friends gave me a chance to catch up on my homework. And I read a pretty good book about a girl with low self-esteem who wants to be with the most popular guy in school but can't find a way to get to him.

Well . . . that's not my problem. I don't have esteem issues. I just kept wanting the girl in the novel to shape up and go talk to the boy she had a crush on.

Heather came into my room on Sunday afternoon. I was painting my toenails. The most awesome blue color

I've ever seen. So awesome I wanted to go barefoot everywhere.

She was in her tennis whites. The short, pleated skirt made her legs look fat. She swung a tennis racket in front of her. "Want to play? We could get a court at Shadyside Park."

I sighed. "I don't think so."

Behind her glasses, her eyes went wide. "Why not? You're not doing anything else."

"I just don't feel like it," I said. "Besides, why do you want to play with me? I beat you every single game."

She spun the racket in her hands. "Just thought we could spend some time together. You know?"

"Well, sorry, but no thanks," I said. Then I added, "Why aren't you spending time with your new best friend, Rose Groban?"

Heather scowled. "Rose has no time for me. She's with Jack all the time now. It's like they're glued together."

I guess she'd gotten tired of Heather even more quickly than I'd thought.

Heather shook her head. "I wanted to tag along with them to the movie theater at the mall last night, and Rose practically told me to get lost. I don't get it. A few days ago, we were friends."

"Sorry," I said. "I've got my own problems."

"Sure you don't want to play? Just one set?"

"I don't think so," I replied, and I returned to brushing color on my toenails.

She turned and stomped out of the room, muttering to herself.

So, Heather was hurt. But I couldn't feel sorry for her. I had my own issues. Besides, Heather had only wanted to get close to Rose to make me angry. She knew that Rose was my enemy. So how could I feel sympathetic now that Rose had dumped her?

So . . . that was the weekend. The highlight was painting my toenails. And now it's Monday after school and I'm at my new job. Yes, Mom made me get a *new* job. She wouldn't get out of my face about the disaster at Lefty's. She said I had to show that I was responsible.

So I'm sitting in this cramped, cluttered office, sitting here behind a gray metal desk with a three-line phone system, a laptop computer, and a special radio unit; I'm a taxi dispatcher.

The red-white-and-blue sign on the wall behind me says ALL-AMERICAN TAXI, and it's shaped like a steering wheel, and there are plaques on all four walls. I guess they are awards the taxi company won from someone. I haven't had time to really examine them.

My uncle David got me this job. And Mom says that makes it double-important that I don't mess it up. Because we don't want to embarrass Uncle David.

I won't mess it up. It's an easy job, much easier than being a waitress. I just answer the phone, then radio the drivers and give them the address of their pickup.

It's mostly quiet. People don't use taxis much in Shadyside. So I can put in my earbuds and listen to music and do my homework and read.

And . . . think of revenge.

Keith called that night, my first day on the job. I hesitated, staring at his name on my phone screen. I hadn't heard from him or seen him in school for days. Actually, I'd forgotten about Keith, just swept him from my mind.

I accepted the call. "Keith? Hi."

"Just calling to say hi," he said. "How's the new job?"

"You heard about it?"

"Yeah. I ran into Heather. She told me you were a taxi mogul now."

I laughed. "A mogul? At ten dollars an hour?"

"So, Poppy, how's it going?"

"All right," I said. "It's a boring job, but it's easy."

"I meant how's it going otherwise?"

I took a breath. Did I really want to talk to Keith? I

couldn't decide. "Keith, why are you calling?"

"I heard about the store robbery joke. Ivy and Jeremy told me about it. It was really mean, Poppy. They feel terrible."

"Yeah. Terrible," I muttered sarcastically.

"The whole thing was crazy," Keith said. "I . . . I just wanted to see if you're okay."

"Nice of you," I said. I wanted to get off the phone. I knew what Keith wanted. He had his *sincere* voice on. And I knew what was coming.

"I wouldn't have gone along with that," he said. "I would have tried to stop them."

"I know how careful you are," I said. "I know you wouldn't—"

"You don't really know me," he interrupted. "You don't really know me at all." Now there was a desperation in his voice. It was strange.

"I have to get off, Keith. I'm not allowed to have personal calls."

"Okay. All right. I just wanted . . . I guess I wanted to say I miss you."

Oh, wow. I didn't want to hurt him. But I didn't want to get back with him, either.

"I'm sorry," I said. I said it kind of coldly so he'd get the message. "Gotta go. Catch you in school."

"But, Poppy, listen. I—"

I clicked off. The taxi phone was ringing. I pictured Keith sitting somewhere, still holding his phone, his face crumpled into a hurt expression.

Maybe he'd finally get the idea this time. We were over.

The time went by slowly. There were a few calls for taxis, but mostly I sat there listening to music and reading *Pride and Prejudice* for English class.

My shift was over at nine. I switched on the automatic call unit, packed my phone and book into my backpack, and wrapped my scarf tighter around my neck. Yes, I even wear a silk scarf to my lonely little job. I just feel safer, more comfortable with a scarf on.

I headed to the taxi garage in back where I parked my car. It's an indoor garage, dimly lit, low, concrete ceilings, kind of spooky, much bigger than it needs to be since the company has only seven taxis.

The sound of my shoes echoed against the stone walls as I walked to my car at the far end. I thought I saw a rat scamper under a parked taxi, a flash of gray. I started to walk faster.

Four taxis were parked in a line in the center spots. That meant three taxis were out on the job. I glimpsed the narrow driveway that led out of the garage.

I was halfway to my car when I heard a cough.

I stopped. And listened. My skin tingled.

I'm not alone.

Someone else is here.

"Who's there?" My voice came out muffled from my sudden fear.

Silence. A ringing silence. No answer.

"Is someone back here?"

I heard a soft scraping sound. The sound of someone trying to walk quietly.

I squinted at the parked taxis. I didn't see anyone. The air in the garage seemed to grow colder.

"Who's there?" I called. "Answer me!"

The silence hung heavily in the air. I could hear someone breathing rapidly. Were they trying to scare me? They were doing a good job of it.

I turned to my car against the back wall. Could I make it there in time to get away?

I took a deep breath and started to run.

And a man stepped out of the shadows to block my path.

"You!" I gasped. "What are *you* doing here?"

34

POPPY NARRATES

I stared in surprise, my legs trembling, my heart pounding, at Lucas, the weird guy from Harlow's store. He stared back at me with those dark eyes that seemed to be jumping around all the time. His brown hair fell in tangles at the sides of his head. The light caught the silver ring in his nose.

He wore a flannel shirt, open to reveal a stained T-shirt underneath, and baggy jeans that hung low enough to show a few inches of his boxer shorts.

As he stared at me, a lopsided smile formed on his pale face.

"Lucas, what are you doing here?" I demanded. My muscles were tight. I was on high alert. Ready to run if I had to. "Did you follow me?"

His smile grew wider. His crazy eyes seemed to penetrate me. His expression, the way he stood, as if ready to stop me, was chilling.

"You . . . have to leave," I choked out. "I mean it. You have to leave now."

I took a sharp intake of breath as he moved toward me.

"But I like you," he whispered.

What?

"Lucas, listen—"

Before I could back away, he was right in front of me, so close I could smell the beer on his breath. "No. Listen—" I started.

He took the ends of my scarf in his hands and began to play with them. "I like you, Poppy," he whispered. "I like you a lot."

"Let go of me!" I screamed. I grabbed his arms hard and shoved him away. As he staggered back, he pulled the scarf off my neck. "Go away, Lucas. Go away!" I cried.

I spun away from him and started to run to my car. I didn't care about the scarf. I just wanted to get away.

I could hear him running after me. I glanced back and saw him waving my scarf in front of him as he ran.

"I like you, Poppy," he called, his words ringing off the concrete walls as if they were all around me, surrounding me. "Don't run away. I like you."

I tugged the car keys from my bag. I was just a few feet away from the car. Could I get inside and lock the door before he caught me?

"Ohhhhh!" I screamed as I fumbled the keys and they flew from my hand. They clattered to the garage floor and bounced toward my car.

I dove for them.

But Lucas was too fast. He dropped to his knees and scooped my keys into his hand.

As I stood over him, gasping for breath, an ugly smile crossed his face. He raised the keys, just out of my reach. "Look what I found. Guess you're not going anywhere."

35

POPPY NARRATES

I swiped my hand forward and made a grab for my keys. He tugged his hand back, and I missed.

Lucas laughed, his crazy eyes flashing, and jumped to his feet. He had my scarf and my keys. The whole thing seemed like a joke to him. That lopsided smile didn't leave his face.

"Give me the keys—" I choked out.

He moved forward and backed me against the side of my car. He pressed himself against me, pushing hard. No way to escape.

I froze in panic. How crazy was he? How dangerous? What was he going to do to me?

I uttered a short cry of surprise when he pressed the

car keys into my hand. "See? I'm a nice guy. I can be a nice guy, too."

I pushed him back. "Just go away, Lucas. Please."

His head drooped. He took a few awkward steps back. Just enough to let me edge to the car door. I pulled it open and practically leaped inside. I saw him wrapping my scarf around one hand. I slammed the door shut and locked it.

My hand shook so hard, it took three tries to press the start button. The car started up with a roar.

I shoved it into reverse. I started to back out of the spot—then slammed the brake hard. Lucas stood behind the car. I watched him in the mirror. He waved my scarf in front of him.

I sent the window rolling down. "Get out of my way! Let me go, Lucas."

He laughed that ugly laugh again. He didn't move.

"Get out of the way. I'll run you over. I swear I will."

"Try it!" he called back.

"Come on, Lucas. Move!"

"Poppy, do you want to go out some time?" he asked.

"Are you crazy?"

"Is that a no?"

I hit the gas pedal and backed the car up, swinging

the wheel, hoping to miss him.

"Whoooooaaah!" He screamed as the car backed into him. I stopped and watched in the mirror as he scrambled onto the trunk. He hunched on his hands and knees on the trunk. I shot the car forward, and he went tumbling off.

I didn't wait to see if he was okay. My tires screeched as I spun the car to the narrow driveway, and I sped out of the garage, deep shudders running down my body, the car squealing from side to side, my trembling hands not really in control.

That creep. That stupid creep.

Did he really ask me out after terrifying me?

He backed me against my car and stole my scarf. And then he asked me out.

Is he totally out of his mind?

Somehow I made it home. I was shaking the whole way and fighting back tears. I didn't want to cry. I was more angry than upset.

I just wanted to get to my room, and close my eyes, and try not to think, and let the shudders end. But Heather stopped me in the living room.

She sat on the couch with her stockinged feet on the coffee table, her laptop balanced on her lap. She looked up from the glow of the screen as I entered the room.

"How was your new job?"

"The job is okay," I said. Then I sighed. "But I had a little problem. That creep from Harlow's store. Lucas. He followed me into the garage behind the office. He . . . he practically attacked me. I think he just wanted to frighten me. I don't know. I don't know what he thought he was doing. He kept saying he *liked* me. It was awful."

I dropped down on the couch beside Heather. I suddenly felt so weary. I guess it was all the adrenaline letting down.

Heather patted my leg. "Wow. That's scary. What did you do?"

"I . . . I almost backed my car over him. It was a nightmare!"

She shook her head. "How awful."

"I—I don't know how dangerous he is," I stammered.

Heather closed her laptop. "Want to hear something weird? Someone at school said they saw Keith hanging out with Lucas. Like they were real buddies or something."

I frowned. "That can't be true. Keith would never hang with a loser like Lucas. That's ridiculous."

"It's what I heard."

"No way. Your friend has got to be kidding. Keith would hate Lucas."

Heather shoved her glasses up on her nose. "Oh. I almost forgot. Ivy called here. She was trying to reach you."

I squinted at my sister. "Ivy called here? Why didn't she call my phone?"

"She said she kept getting voicemail. Like you wouldn't pick up."

I pulled my phone out of my bag. It was dead. Completely out of power. Probably why Ivy didn't get through.

"I don't want to talk to her anyway," I said.

"She told me she misses you. She wants to make up with you."

"It isn't going to happen," I said. "All of my friends are dead to me. They totally messed with my head, and I'm going to pay them back."

"Poppy, Ivy has been your friend for years," Heather said. "And now you're planning some kind of revenge against her? What are you going to do?"

"Something terrible," I said. "I don't know what yet. But it will be terrible."

36

IVY NARRATES

I sat on Jeremy's lap, the lights dimmed in the den. I had the music from the wall speakers on low so I wouldn't disturb my parents, who had already gone to bed.

Jeremy held me tightly, and our mouths pressed together in a long kiss that was already making me breathless. I took a short break, then slid my hands over his cheeks and pulled his face back to mine.

I wondered if he could tell that I had something else on my mind. I kept glancing at the clock on the mantel and thinking about my ten o'clock visitor.

Yes, I'd invited Poppy over after her job at the taxi company. I'd finally reached her and finally got her to agree to let me apologize. I was nervous, totally stressed because I didn't know what I was going to say.

The prank we played on Poppy was mean and stupid. Why had we let Jack persuade us that it would be funny, that Poppy would think it was funny? We should have stood up to him. We should have told him he was going too far.

Also, Jack had never told us that Rose was involved. We never knew that she was behind the whole thing, that Jack was just doing it for her.

We actually thought Jack and Poppy were together. We had no idea that Jack was just playing with her, that he was loyal to Rose the whole time.

We were stupid. What were we thinking?

And now, I really couldn't concentrate on Jeremy. I had to figure out what to say to Poppy, my oldest friend.

I ran my hand through Jeremy's hair. Then I pulled away. "You'll never guess who dropped by," I said. "Keith. You just missed him."

Jeremy blinked. "Keith? He was here? Why?"

"I'm not sure. I think he wanted to talk about Poppy. He was only here for a few minutes. It was totally awkward."

"Yeah. Weird," Jeremy agreed. He leaned forward and kissed me again.

"You've got to go," I said. "Sorry. I want to talk to Poppy alone."

He blinked a few times. "Poppy?"

I nodded. "I told you. She'll be here any minute."

He put his hands on my waist and helped me to my feet. I straightened the short skirt I was wearing over black tights.

"Ivy, what are you going to say to her?"

I shrugged. "Don't know. Guess I'll just drop to my knees and beg her forgiveness."

He stood up. "Don't you want me to stay? We can both apologize together."

"No." I gave him a gentle push. "Get going. This has to be between Poppy and me. If I can get her to forgive me, she'll forgive you, too."

Jeremy kissed me on the cheek, then turned and made his way to the front door. I walked to the bathroom across from my room and used the mirror to straighten my hair. I brushed out a few tangles and swept it one way, then the other. I don't know why I was spending so much time on my hair. Poppy didn't care what I looked like.

The sound of the doorbell made me jump. I dropped my hairbrush onto the floor. As I walked to the front door, I could feel my hands go cold and my stomach tighten.

I suddenly wished I had planned what I was going to say. But Poppy and I had been friends for so long, I thought we could just talk the way we always had. Comfortable, like old friends.

Wow, was I wrong.

When I pulled the front door open, there she was, in a dark top, a gray patterned scarf hanging loosely from her neck, and black short shorts, her face already twisted into an angry scowl. She didn't say hello or anything. She just asked if she could use my bathroom.

I led her down the hall to the bathroom. We didn't say a word to each other as we walked. I waited for her in my room, perched on the edge of my bed. She was gone a long time. When she finally appeared in the doorway, she said, "I can't stay."

"Please," I said, motioning to the green leather armchair against the window. "Just sit down for a minute so I can apologize to you."

She stood stubbornly in the doorway. "Apologize? Are you joking?"

"Please. Give me a chance." I motioned to the chair again.

I knew Poppy had a temper. I was in Lefty's the night she smashed the cheeseburger into Rose Groban's face. But she also could be warm and funny, and was the most enthusiastic person I knew. If she was into something or someone, she was in all the way.

So far, I wasn't feeling any warmth.

"I just want to say—" I started.

She raised a hand. "Save it."

"You're not even going to give me a chance to say I'm sorry?"

She shook her head. "You just said it. Can I go now?"

I jumped to my feet and took a few steps toward her. "Why are you acting like this? How long have we been friends, Poppy? How long? Doesn't that count for anything?"

"No, it doesn't," she said. She stepped forward, as if to challenge me. "What kind of friend betrays another friend?"

"Betrays?" I cried.

"Betrays and humiliates. How could you go along with that prank, Ivy? How could you? You had to know it would be the worst night of my life."

"I . . . I didn't know," I stammered. "Jack had us all convinced—"

"Shut up about Jack," she snapped. "Just shut up. You have a brain. No one forced you to do it. Jack didn't force you. You agreed to it. You agreed to it and you know it."

"Poppy, listen—" She had her fists clenched. Was she really planning to fight me? To hurt me? "You're right," I said, my throat suddenly tight. "It was terrible. I was terrible. I should have known better. But I want to apologize now. I want us to get past it. Can't we start all new?"

She laughed a cold laugh.

"Pitiful," she said. "Start all new? Ha. That's pitiful." She stepped up close to me. She lowered her gaze. I thought I saw tears on her cheeks. "It hurt too much, Ivy. It hurt too much. I thought . . . I thought you were my friends. But I saw what being a friend meant to you all."

"I . . . I can be a good friend." I didn't want to cry, but hot tears were running down *my* cheeks now. "Poppy, I can be a good friend."

She spun away. "I . . . I don't think so."

I stood there, trembling, tears rolling down my face, and listened to her footsteps as she made her way down the hall. I heard the front door slam, and I still didn't move.

We had been so close, such good pals. And I had ruined it by going along with Jack's stupid prank. How was I supposed to know that he and Rose had dreamed it up? How were any of us to know?

I stood there in my room with my fists clenched and my head spinning. My stomach felt like I had swallowed a rock. I wanted to climb into bed and pull the covers over my head.

"I guess that's it," I said aloud. "I've lost my best friend."

I wiped the tears on my cheeks with both hands. Then I started to pull off my clothes. I knew there was only one way to calm myself. The only thing that ever calms me is a good, long shower.

I crossed the hall to my bathroom and got my shower going. It takes a while for the water to get hot. I fluffed my hair out with my hands and grabbed the shampoo bottle I keep on my sink.

I kept remembering Poppy and me having good times together. I couldn't keep the pictures from my mind. I saw us riding an elephant at the circus when we were ten. And baking apple pies all by ourselves in her kitchen when we were older.

I remembered what we wore at our junior-high prom, and the two geeks who were our dates. I saw us going for our driver's test together downtown.

I stepped into the shower. I needed the hot water to splash the memories away. I let the water soak my hair. I lowered my head and raised the back of my hair to the steaming water.

Yes . . . Whenever I got stressed out, this was the only thing that ever calmed me.

I squeezed a puddle of shampoo onto my palm and rubbed it into my hair. Not enough. I poured out more shampoo and smoothed it down the length of my hair.

The shampoo had a coconut aroma. I shut my eyes and pretended I was down in a tropical island, with palm trees and coconuts and—

"Hey—!"

I cried out when I felt the tingle at the top of my head. *What's up with that?*

The tingle quickly spread. It became a burning sensation.

"Oh, wait. Oh, wait."

I raised my hands to the top of my head. The pain spread over my scalp and down the back of my neck. "Owwwww." It hurt. It really hurt. And it was growing more intense.

I grabbed at my hair—*and a thick clump came off in my hand.*

What is happening?

My head burned as if it was on fire. I lowered my glance and saw clumps of my hair on the shower floor.

"Nooooooo!" A scream burst from my mouth. I shut off the water. Stepped out of the shower. Hands clamped to my burning, throbbing head, I stumbled to the mirror.

Big bald spots. My scalp flaming red. The sink filled with my hair.

"Oh, it hurts. It hurts."

I tugged out another clump.

Was something wrong with the shampoo?

My head was burning . . . my hands were burning . . . burning . . . on fire.

I couldn't stand it. I couldn't think. The pain was burning down to my brain.

I started to scream. "Help me! Please! Someone? Anyone? *Please*—help me!"

37

JEREMY NARRATES

My asthma was kicking up, and I was using my inhaler when the phone rang. It was Ivy, screaming and crying. I thought something was wrong with my phone or maybe my ears because I couldn't understand a word she was saying, she was so out of control—I mean, hysterical.

"I'm at Shadyside General."

I finally understood. "The hospital?" I said. "Why? What's wrong? Are you okay?"

"No, I'm *not* okay. I'm ruined, Jeremy. I'm in horrible pain. My head—it's burning. I—I—She tried to kill me."

I pressed the phone to my ear. I couldn't believe I was hearing this. Ivy didn't sound like herself. I actually thought it might be a joke. We've all been playing jokes on each other, and I just couldn't imagine what she was screaming about.

"Please . . . take a breath," I pleaded. "I can't understand. What happened? Tell me. Who tried to . . . kill you?"

"I'm totally bald!" she screamed. "My hair—it's gone. Do you understand that? I'm bald, and I have burns all over my scalp and hands."

I swallowed. My mouth was suddenly dry. "But—why? How?"

"The police . . . they were at my house," Ivy said. "My shampoo. They examined my shampoo. They found *acid* in my shampoo." She burst into loud sobs.

My brain was spinning. How was this possible? Who would do a thing like that? It had to be a mistake. It couldn't have happened. Ivy had such a thing about her hair. No one would do that. No one.

I waited for her to stop sobbing. "What did the doctors say, Ivy?" I asked. "Are you all right?"

"I have burns all over my head. They're going to treat them. They say I can go home tomorrow."

"I . . . I don't know what to say. I—"

"It had to be Poppy."

I swallowed again. "Huh? Poppy? What do you mean?"

"She did it. She put the acid in the shampoo, Jeremy. I know what she's doing. I'm sure of it."

"Please try to calm down, Ivy," I said. "You sound like you're berserk or something. I mean—"

"Berserk? Of course I'm berserk. I lost my hair, Jeremy. All of it. She tried to kill me. Don't you see? Poppy is getting some kind of crazy revenge."

I couldn't believe it. "Poppy is your friend," I said. "Yeah, she's angry about the robbery prank, but she wouldn't—"

"I told the police about her. It had to be her." She started to sob again.

I didn't know what to say. Acid in her shampoo? What a vicious attack. It could have blinded Ivy. It could have killed her. Could Poppy have done that?

I've known Poppy forever. Sure, she gets angry. She has a temper. She's an enthusiastic person. She never goes halfway. But she isn't a killer. And she isn't vicious. She would never hurt Ivy like that, even if she's angry at her.

Or am I wrong? Poppy did *swear revenge that night.*

"Jeremy, sorry. I just keep crying. I can't stop." Ivy's voice shook me from my thoughts. "Can you come here?

Can you come to the hospital?"

I let out a long whoosh of air. I wanted to be with Ivy, but I knew I couldn't.

"I can't leave the house," I said. "I'm really sorry. My asthma is bad, and my inhaler is nearly empty. I have to be really careful, Ivy. I'm not breathing very well."

A long silence. I could hear her breathing. "I see," she said finally. "Well . . . hope you're okay."

"I'll call you tomorrow," I said. "I'll come see you at your house."

"I don't want anyone to see me. Ever again. My head looks like a burned marshmallow." She was crying and talking at the same time.

"I'm so sorry," I said. "The police will catch whoever did it. Meanwhile, maybe you should get some rest," I said.

"I've got to go. The doctors are here." She clicked off.

I sat there for a while at the edge of my bed. Ugly pictures ran through my mind, visions of Ivy without her beautiful hair, Ivy with her head burned and bandaged.

I reached for the inhaler. The horror of her news was making my breathing more difficult. I realized I was making loud wheezing sounds with each breath, and each breath was a struggle.

I squeezed the inhaler once, twice. It was nearly empty. I knew I had to calm down and get my breathing under control.

I changed for bed, turned off the lights, and slid under the covers. The streetlamp outside my open bedroom window sent an angled pattern of light onto the wall. I turned on my side, away from the light, and shut my eyes.

It took a long time to get to sleep. I kept hearing Ivy's angry, shrill voice, and her sobs. I finally drifted off into a deep, dreamless sleep.

I don't know how long I slept. I was awakened by a loud buzzing sound. At first, I thought it was my phone. But the rasping sound rose and fell and seemed to surround me.

I cried out when something swiped against my forehead. I felt another bump at the back of my head.

I clicked on the light—and screamed.

The room was filled with big flying, buzzing insects. What were they? I swatted one off the top of my head. I kept blinking myself awake, blinking until I could focus on the swarming creatures.

Hornets!

Dozens of black hornets, swooping in a swarm up to

my ceiling, then down again, circling my room, buzzing angrily. I sat up. Struggled to pull myself out of bed. But my feet tangled in the bed sheet and I fell to the floor.

How did they get in? I glanced and saw that the window was shut. But hadn't it been open when I went to bed?

"Ow!" I uttered a cry at the first sting. My arm throbbed. And then another angry pinch, a pinprick of pain, as a hornet stung the back of my neck.

"Ow!" I wrestled with the bedsheet. Managed to free myself. "Ow." A sting on the middle of my back, right through my T-shirt.

I stood up. And they swarmed around me, circling me, flying inches from my body, buzzing louder . . . louder.

"Help!" I cried weakly.

The hornets were so thick over my face, I couldn't see past them. I saw only the glistening black of their fat bodies as they circled. I tried swinging both arms, trying to bat them away. But they clung to my arms and began to sting. The buzzing grew lower as the angry creatures attached themselves to my chest, my legs, my face.

I twisted and turned and shouted and cried as they swarmed over me, stinging . . . stinging . . . my skin ringing in pain, the pain so overwhelming, I couldn't see, I couldn't think. I was being buried under the swarm, under their vicious bites . . . buried . . .

Oh, help. Please. I can't brush them off. I can't swat them away.

I can't . . . I can't breathe . . . can't breathe . . . can't breathe.

38

POPPY CONTINUES THE STORY

I saw the black-and-white patrol car pull up our driveway. I watched them climb out of the car, two of them. I opened the front door before they rang the bell.

One cop was tall and thin—I mean very thin—with a tuft of short red hair on his pale face. Standing at the front door, he reminded me of a matchstick. He said his name was Officer Raap. He had a deep voice that made his Adam's apple go up and down in his skinny neck. It looked like a small animal in his throat.

The other cop was Benny Kline, Manny's brother. I'd never seen him with such a stern expression on his face. And when he spoke, he kept his eyes on me as if trying to dig into my brain. "Can we come in?"

What was I going to say? *No? Sorry, I'm busy watching* Dr. Who.

I led them into the living room. Mom and Heather came into the room, and everyone arranged themselves as awkwardly as possible. Because it has to be awkward when you have two police officers in your living room, questioning you.

Benny and Raap sat together on the couch. Mom and Heather perched on chairs on either side, and I dropped onto a leather ottoman across from everyone. It was too low and made my knees come up almost to my face.

I didn't really care. Keith told me about Ivy and Jeremy being taken to the hospital. I was horribly upset and worried about my friends and not prepared to answer questions about the awful things someone had done to them.

Both cops dropped their caps on the coffee table. Raap scratched his short red hair. Benny's belly poked at the front of his uniform. "We're talking to all your friends," he started. "Everyone in your group."

"You want to question Poppy about Ivy and Jeremy?" Mom chimed in. She had her hands clasped tightly in her lap, and she kept shifting in her chair, unable to get comfortable.

"Yes, we do," Raap said in his surprisingly deep voice. "You visited Ivy last night, Poppy. Yes?"

I nodded. "Yes. I did my shift at the taxi company where I work. Then I went home. Then to Ivy's."

"And where did you go after you saw Ivy?"

"Well . . . nowhere, really. I drove around for a while. I was upset and I didn't want to just go home."

Benny leaned forward. "You said you were upset. Can you tell us what you were upset about?"

"Well . . . Ivy and I . . . we were friends for a long time. And now we aren't friends anymore. Because I'm furious at her. And she thought she could just apologize, and that would be that. But she and my other friends did a very mean thing to me. And . . . and . . . I'm not ready to forgive them."

The two cops exchanged glances. Raap typed something with two fingers onto an iPad mini. They sat there silently for a few seconds, their heads down.

Then Benny said, "I know you were very angry about the robbery prank. I was there at Harlow's store, remember? I was there, Poppy, and I heard you say you would get revenge . . . that you would pay them all back for embarrassing you like that." His dark eyes locked on mine. "Did I remember that right?"

I couldn't deny it. "Well, yes," I started. "I went a

little crazy. I was so hurt . . . so humiliated . . . I just lashed out, let my anger take control. Yes, you're right, Benny. I did say that. I did say that I'd get my revenge. But, of course, when I calmed down, I realized that was . . . silly."

They both stared at me, studying me. I suddenly felt cold. I wrapped my arms around myself. Mom fidgeted on her chair. I could see she was totally tense. Heather looked on, a silent observer.

"So you decided *not* to get revenge on your friends?" Raap said. "Are you sure? You abandoned the idea?"

I nodded. "Yes, I'm sure."

"Someone put acid in Ivy's shampoo bottle," Raap said, not lowering his gaze. "Do you know anything about that, Poppy?"

"No way," I said, feeling the tears well in my eyes. "No way. I would never do something like that. Poor Ivy. All she cared about was her beautiful hair."

"And you don't have any idea who might have put the acid into the shampoo bottle?" Raap asked.

I shook my head. "No."

"Are you accusing my daughter of this hideous crime?" Mom broke in, her voice tight and shrill.

"No. Not at all," Benny answered quickly. "We're

just gathering information. That's all."

I shuddered. "I don't know anything about acid," I said. "I'm telling the truth."

Suddenly, Heather turned to me. "Poppy, what was that stuff you used to clean that old jewelry of Grandma's?" she said. "Remember? Down in the basement?"

Both officers reacted in surprise. They both looked at Heather as if they hadn't noticed her before. Then they turned back to me and waited for me to answer.

"I—I don't know," I said in a whisper.

"The instructions said to use rubber gloves to protect your skin, didn't it?" she kept on.

Thank you, Heather. Thank you, dear sister. Now I can see that they both suspect me. They think they've solved their case.

"I used a cleaner that contains hydrochloric acid to clean my grandmother's gold jewelry," I told them. "The bottle . . . it's in the basement. I never took it out of the basement."

Raap started to his feet. "Can we see it? Mrs. Miller, is it okay if we go down to your basement?"

Mom just shrugged. "I guess." She stood up. "I'm sure Poppy is telling the truth. The acid was just for cleaning jewelry."

"It's pretty powerful acid for jewelry," Raap said, his eyes on me.

"Not for gold," I said. "The woman at the store told me it's best for gold."

I led the way to the basement stairs. I noticed that Heather was avoiding my gaze. I hoped she was embarrassed for revealing I had a bottle of acid. I didn't really know her motive. Had she just blurted it out without thinking?

Was she actually trying to get me in trouble?

The air in the basement was warm. We ducked under the low ceiling. "The acid bottle is on the shelf over there. In my dad's old workshop," I said.

Mom and Heather held back. I led the two officers to the shelf where I kept it.

My eyes glanced up and down the shelves. My heart started to beat a pounding rhythm. I squinted and let my eyes go over each item on the shelf—paint cans, brushes, piles of rags, cans of shellac.

"Oh," I gasped. "I . . . don't believe it. The bottle is gone."

39

POPPY CONTINUES

"Maybe you put it on a different shelf," Benny suggested.

"Maybe." My legs were shaking. "Maybe . . . uh . . . I finished the bottle and threw it in the trash."

Raap narrowed his eyes at me. "Do you remember doing that?"

"No," I said honestly. "No. I remember putting the bottle on this shelf."

Everyone in the basement was staring at me now, including Mom and Heather. Raap stepped up to the shelf and examined it himself. "Hydrochloric acid is powerful," he said as he searched. "It'll burn right through human skin on contact."

I imagined Ivy in the hospital, her whole head covered

in bandages. "How bad are Ivy's burns?" I asked. "I haven't been to the hospital."

"Her face wasn't burned," Raap said. "Only her head and hands. If her hair grows back, it will cover most of the scars from the burns."

"*If* her hair grows back?" I uttered. I had a sick feeling in the pit of my stomach. A sob escaped my throat. "She was so proud of her hair. It was like . . . like her whole personality."

"You wanted revenge, and you had the acid," Raap said, almost in a whisper. "You can't explain why the acid bottle isn't here. Did you use it, Poppy?"

"No. Of course not!" I shouted.

"Does my daughter need a lawyer?" Mom demanded. "Are you charging her with this crime?"

"I'm not crazy!" I cried, before either cop could answer her. "Yes, I got angry at my friends. Yes, I said a lot of angry things. But I'm not a psycho. I'm not insane. I don't go burning my friends' hair off. I don't! *I don't!*"

I was screaming at the top of my lungs. Mom put her hands on my shoulders and then slid her arms down into a hug from behind, trying to calm me. My whole body was shaking, more with anger than with fright.

"Can we go upstairs?" Officer Raap was deliberately

keeping his voice low and calm. I hated him. I hated him because I could read his thoughts. He thought he had solved the Case of the Acid in the Shampoo. A missing acid bottle was all it took. Case closed.

Perhaps he would get acid samples from Ivy's scalp. He'd match the samples to hydrochloric acid, and if they matched, it would be obvious that I was the culprit; I was the psycho who sneaked into Ivy's bathroom and mixed the shampoo solution.

As we headed back up to the living room, I had a sudden jolt of memory. I *had* used Ivy's bathroom last night. I asked Ivy for the bathroom as soon as I arrived. I remembered that now, and I bet Ivy remembered it, too.

Case closed. I'm guilty.

As we took our old places in the living room, I watched for Officer Raap to whip out the handcuffs.

I saw Mom fidgeting in her chair, clasping and unclasping her hands. Heather had this blank look on her face, like maybe she was somewhere else. Or maybe she was thinking this couldn't be happening.

That was my thought exactly, and of course, it *was* happening, and I was looking like a crazed psycho who would burn my friend's head off because somehow that acid bottle just vanished from the shelf.

"Mrs. Miller, are you okay?" Benny asked. Both cops were watching her carefully.

"Not really," she said. "I know that my daughter would never do anything like this, and I just can't believe that you two are questioning her—"

"We're questioning everyone in their circle of friends," Benny offered. "Even my brother."

"Manny?" I couldn't hide my surprise. "Manny's the last person I'd question. Manny is definitely not the killer type."

"Who is?" Raap demanded.

The question caught me by surprise and I gasped.

"Poppy, do you know anyone who would want to harm Ivy?" he demanded.

"Besides me?" I replied. "No. I . . . I don't. I—"

I heard a buzzing sound. Raap raised his palm, signaling for quiet. He pulled his phone to his ear. His eyes grew wide as he listened. He nodded once, twice, and muttered something I couldn't hear.

Benny's big body tensed. He stared at his partner, listening to what he could hear of the conversation. Mom sat forward on the edge of her chair. Heather started playing with her stringy hair, twisting and untwisting a strand.

Finally, Raap clicked off. He lowered his phone slowly to his lap, his expression thoughtful. "Afraid I have bad news," he said finally, his face suddenly so pale it was ghostlike.

Benny shook his head and lowered his eyes. He knew what Raap was about to say.

Raap narrowed his eyes at me. "Your friend Jeremy has died in the hospital. He never recovered consciousness after the hornet stings."

"Oh nooooo." A shuddering gasp escaped my open mouth. I covered my face with both hands. I couldn't stop the sobs that wracked my body. "Noooo. Oh noooo."

I felt hands grip my rocking shoulders. I lowered my hands enough to see Mom trying to wrap me in an awkward hug. "This can't be happening," I choked out, my face soaked with tears. "These are my friends. This can't be happening."

The two officers were on their feet. "So sorry," Benny said. "So sorry. This was a terrible crime. But we'll find the culprit."

I covered my face again. I knew they still suspected me. But Benny's words helped make me feel a little better. Mom held on to my shoulders. She motioned for Heather to show the two cops to the door.

"We'll need to talk again," Raap said. "Right now, we'd better get to Shadyside General."

I heard the door close behind them. "I'm going to my room," Heather said. "I . . . don't know what to say. I'm totally messed up. My brain . . . it just won't wrap itself around this. Sorry, Poppy."

Mom squeezed my shoulders. "Look at me, Poppy," she said in a low whisper. "Turn around and look at me."

I lowered my hands from my face. My cheeks were hot and soaked in tears. To my surprise, Mom's expression wasn't sympathetic. It was stern.

She locked her eyes on mine. "I need you to tell me the truth, Poppy," she said.

I blinked tears from my eyes. "Huh? The truth?"

Mom nodded. "Yes, I want the truth. You *know* those hornets came from my lab."

40

KEITH NARRATES

I went to the hospital to see Ivy, and Manny was already in her room. I felt a little awkward because I didn't know if they had told her the news about Jeremy.

But it didn't take long to see that Ivy knew, because she had a handkerchief up to her face and was crying so hard, a nurse came hurrying into the room.

"Do you need something to calm yourself?" she asked. She was a large, middle-aged woman, and her green uniform pants fell baggy all around her. Some wisps of gray hair hung around her face.

Ivy was already hooked up to an IV, a clear hose attached to a bag of some kind of liquid that was hanging from a pole beside her bed. It was injected into her wrist, so she had to hold the handkerchief she was crying into in her left hand.

Ivy shook her head no. Waved the nurse away. "I . . . I don't want anything." Her voice was all cramped and fluttery. It didn't sound like Ivy.

I kept staring at the bandages that covered most of her scalp and came down to the back of her neck. Her hands were wrapped too. They looked like mummy bandages, and I couldn't help it—I had this thought that Ivy was all ready for Halloween.

Hospitals freak me out. You can't control your thoughts in a hospital. You think crazy things you shouldn't, like Ivy being a mummy for Halloween. And you think frightening things . . . like, you think about people dying. You can smell it in a hospital. That sharp, sour smell. It's death.

I've thought about death a lot since my family moved to a house on Fear Street. Of course, I heard the stories of the evil that seems to hang over that street. I've tried to laugh it off. Ridiculous stories.

But I have to admit I've felt the darkness. Something frightening lurking inside me that wasn't there before we moved.

I spent some time in a hospital. No one knows it. But I did. And I never wanted to return. I never wanted to be hospitalized again.

It sounds so impossible to me now that I OD'd on the cough medicine in Dad's medicine cabinet. What was I doing in there in the first place? And what was wrong with me that I'd thought it would be a good idea to drink down two bottles of the stuff?

What had I been trying to prove?

I'd never answered the question. I don't even know what exactly was in those bottles. But the next thing I knew I was in a hospital bed, and my brain was on Mars or in a deep, dark sewer somewhere. Anywhere but where it should be.

And how long did it take me to come back to consciousness?

My parents told the high school I was visiting an uncle overseas. No one knew that I was lying in a hospital bed, yammering insane things, jabbering and drooling, my mind completely blown to bits.

It was when I'd finally begun to think like me that I'd decided to pull back. I'd decided that it wasn't cool. There was no advantage in being a rebel or a trouble-maker. I guess that was the start of my new personality. Good guy Keith. Boring, good guy Keith.

Well, face it, after my mind almost slipped away from me forever, I was afraid not to be boring.

No one knows this. I thought I could confide in Poppy. I thought Poppy and I could share our biggest secrets. But I was wrong. And I am glad that I never shared my hospital story with her. She wasn't deserving of my confidences. She wasn't worth the time I spent with her.

I miss her and I hate her.

It's as simple as that.

"We just came to say hi," Manny said.

Ivy was so torn to pieces, I don't think she heard him.

"Ivy, when are you going home?" Manny asked, trying to get some kind of response.

Ivy choked out an answer, but I couldn't understand it. I kept staring at the mummy bandages. The poor girl. Her head must hurt so much.

Manny stood up and motioned for me to follow. It wasn't a good time to be visiting.

The nurse returned. "Dr. Mahoney thinks you need to rest," she said to Ivy. She opened a small case and removed a hypodermic needle. "I'm sorry, but your visitors should leave now."

Manny and I were already at the door. "We'll come back," Manny said.

"Hope you feel better," I said. Lame. But what else could I say?

Manny and I made our way down the long hall, past room after room of sick people. The smell was sharp and piney. Like toilet cleaner.

We both took long strides, eager to get out of there. We didn't talk till we were outside. Manny let out a long whoosh of breath. "Whoa. Talk about messed up," he muttered.

I nodded. "Sick. Totally sick."

He motioned to the parking lot. "Want a ride to school?"

I thought for a moment. "I'm skipping out today. I don't really feel like school." I stepped off the front stairs. "Catch you later, dude."

What I really wanted to do was go home and make a few new cuts in my shoulder. That would make me feel better. I knew it would.

41

POPPY NARRATES

"I know the hornets came from my lab," Mom said. "I need an explanation from you, Poppy."

My mouth dropped open. I stared at her. I suddenly felt as if she was a stranger, someone I'd never seen before. "Are you . . . Are you *accusing* me?" I stammered.

"Are you denying it?" she replied, challenging me.

I felt so hurt and angry at the same time. "Mom . . . I never . . . I wouldn't . . ." I stumbled over the words. "Jeremy is d-dead," I stuttered. "Do you think I'm the one who killed him?"

She uttered a sigh and rubbed her forehead as if she had one of her migraines. "I don't know what to think, Poppy. I know that those hornets could only have come from one place. I know that the police won't have any trouble tracing them to my lab."

She kept her eyes covered, massaging her temples. "The truth is, I should tell them. I should tell them *right now* where the hornets came from."

"Mom, look at me," I said. I grabbed her arm and pulled her hand away from her face. "Look at me. Read my lips. I didn't take the hornets. I didn't put the acid in Ivy's shampoo. I didn't do those things, Mom. And you should know me well enough not to accuse me."

A sob escaped my throat. "Do you have any idea how much you have just hurt me?"

She thought for a moment. I could see her eyes sliding back and forth as she concentrated. "I know you have a temper, Poppy. We've talked about it. We've had to deal with it several times. We both know—"

I let go of her arm and stepped back. "You're not going to stop—are you? You're going to keep on accusing me? Even though I told you I didn't do those things to my two friends."

"Okay, okay." She gestured with both hands. I suddenly saw fear in her eyes. "Let's deal with this, Poppy. Let's think about this." She pulled me to the couch and pushed me onto the cushion. She didn't sit down beside me. She started pacing back and forth in front of me.

"Mom, please—"

She waved a hand for me to be quiet. "Listen Poppy, if you didn't do it, someone else is out to hurt your friends, right?"

"Right," I whispered.

"They're out to hurt everyone in your group," she continued, crossing her arms in front of her. "So what makes you think you won't be next?"

"Huh?" The thought hadn't occurred to me.

"You could be next," Mom said. "Don't you see? We . . . we have to lock all the windows and doors. You have to be careful when you go out. Maybe . . . maybe you should quit your job."

I jumped to my feet. "Quit my job? But, Mom—"

"Someone killed Jeremy. Someone attacked your best friend. Do you think they'll stop there? Don't you think you're on the list? Why didn't you think of that?" She narrowed her eyes at me, suspicious. "Why aren't you . . . scared?"

"I—I don't know," I stammered. A chill rolled down my back. "I guess you're right. I guess I should be afraid. And Manny. He should be afraid. And Jack."

Jack . . .

He hadn't said a word to me since the night of the fake robbery. I'd seen him at school, hanging all over Rose, teasing her and kissing her, and draping himself all over her and not caring who was watching. Whenever he passed me in the hall, he pretended he didn't see me.

What a creep.

Was Jack afraid? Was he afraid he might be next? I hoped he was afraid. I guess it was sick, but I hoped he was totally afraid.

That kind of thinking didn't help, I know. But you can't control what you think about when you're under such terrible strain and pressure.

"Did you call Ivy?" Mom's voice broke into my thoughts.

"No. I . . . uh . . . texted her. I tried to call, several times, but she won't take my calls."

"You should try again, Poppy."

"You don't get it, Mom. She thinks I did it. She thinks I tried to kill her. I'm sure she thinks I killed Jeremy. She's not going to take my calls. Not ever again."

I spun away from her and stomped to my room and threw myself on my stomach onto the bed. I shut my eyes and pressed my face into the bedcover.

I tried to get my thoughts in order. I tried to clear

my mind and *think*, just think. I had to force my swirling emotions into the background. All the anger and fear and confusion—it all had to go so that I stood a chance of figuring out what was happening here.

I thought about the hornets. The big insects that Mom was studying. She told me they were more aggressive than normal, and she was trying to find out why. I pictured them. And then I pictured a swarm of them.

I tried to imagine what it would be like to open my eyes and find them buzzing and swirling and flying around my room, hovering low, circling me with their loud anger. And then attacking me. Attaching themselves to my body, my skin, and stinging . . . stinging . . . stinging until every part of me throbbed with unbearable pain.

I had only seen the hornets once, that day I visited Mom's lab. That day I visited Mom's lab with Keith.

Keith.

Wait a minute. Keith was there that day.

I pushed myself up from the bedcover. I sat up with a shivering jerk. *Keith was with me. Keith saw the hornets, too.*

Did this mean anything? My thoughts were sending chills down my back.

I pictured quiet, careful Keith. Could he be the one

who'd attacked Ivy and Jeremy?

Keith?

I knew he'd never liked my friends. But that was no reason to go after them.

Keith . . . He'd acted so weird when I broke up with him. At first, he acted as if his life was over. Then he became angry. So angry he frightened me.

Yes. Yes. I'd put it out of my mind. But Keith had even threatened me. Nothing specific. I couldn't really remember what he'd said.

Then he'd looked about to cry. He'd hurried away. Afterward, he kept calling and texting. He hadn't given up. I had to be really mean to him to convince him to stop and leave me alone.

Was Keith getting revenge now? Revenge on me by attacking my friends and making it look as if I was the culprit?

Suddenly, the thought didn't seem so crazy.

I woke with a start. I glanced at the clock. Where had the day gone? It had whirred by in a blur. I must have fallen asleep. I didn't even realize it.

The phone was in my trembling hand before I even noticed it. I was shaking so hard, it took three tries to punch Keith's number. It rang and rang, and no voice-mail message came on.

It was late. Maybe he was asleep. Maybe he couldn't hear his phone. I let it ring for a long time. Then I clicked off, squeezing the phone in my hand, my thoughts flying crazily around me.

It's late, but I have to see him. I won't sleep tonight unless I confront him.

A few minutes later, I was in the car. My hand trembled as I started it up. I took a deep breath, hoping to stop my heart from beating so hard.

Was this an insane idea? Thinking of Keith as the attacker?

I didn't care how insane it sounded. I had to know the answer.

I left the headlights off. Mom and Heather had gone to bed, and I didn't want either of them to know I was going out this late. I didn't want to hear the millions of questions Mom would ask.

I released the brake and let the car back slowly down the driveway—and almost backed into a dark car parked directly across the street.

I braked hard and avoided a collision. There usually wasn't a car parked there. I turned the wheel and maneuvered away from it. Switched on my headlights.

And in the sudden bright light I saw someone in the parked car. I saw a face behind the steering wheel. And recognized him immediately.

Lucas.

Lucas, pale in the circle of light from my headlights. Lucas, staring out at me, not moving, just staring. Parked in front of my house . . . Lucas . . . Waiting for *what*?

42

POPPY CONTINUES

I squealed down the street. *No way* I was going to confront that creep. I drove for two blocks, still seeing his face in front of me. Then I pulled to the curb and raised my phone.

I dialed 911. After one ring, a woman's voice came on.

"There's someone stalking me. Someone parked across from my house," I blurted out. "He—He—"

She spoke softly and smoothly, trying to calm me down enough to give her the information. I finally managed to tell her my address. I described Lucas and told her he was sitting in a small, dark car. She promised to send a patrol car. "Where are you?" she asked.

"Uh . . . driving somewhere," I said. "To a friend's

house." I clicked off. I glanced in my rearview mirror. A car was approaching. The headlights swept into my car from the back window.

Lucas? Lucas following me?

I froze. *Will he stop his car beside mine? What should I do?*

I let out a long whoosh of air as the car drove right past. It was an SUV, not Lucas's car. Not Lucas.

I sat there a minute or so, getting myself together. Then I lowered my foot to the gas and began to drive toward Keith's house.

Lucas's pale face and his crazy dancing eyes stayed with me. I knew he was weird and I knew he could be violent. And I knew he had a thing for me.

So . . . was it possible that Lucas was going after my friends for some sick, twisted reason? I'd nearly run him over in the taxi garage after work. Was he planning to attack me, too? Mom was right. Whoever was doing this would definitely have me on the list.

I could be the next to die.

Was it that sick creep, Lucas?

I shook my head hard, trying to force his face from my mind. Trying to shake him away so maybe the shudders would stop running down my body.

But I was still shaking when I turned onto Fear Street. Overhanging trees made the night even darker.

Keith's house was in the middle of the block. I eased the car up the gravel driveway. The crunching of the tires on the gravel sounded so loud against the silence outside the car.

The house is a long, low ranch style that stretches at the top of a sloping lawn. It was dark except for a yellow light on the far-right end. The family room, I thought.

A gust of cool wind greeted me as I climbed out of the car. It felt good on my hot cheeks. My legs were shaky as I climbed the front stoop and knocked on the door.

I can't believe I came here to accuse Keith of murdering Jeremy. This is all so unbelievable.

Unbelievable—but happening just the same.

I knocked a little harder. I didn't want to ring the bell and wake everyone up.

I heard footsteps inside. And then the door was pulled open, and Mrs. Carter, Keith's mom, stared out at me with sleepy eyes. She was in a long, loose housedress. She carried a TV remote in one hand.

She squinted at me. "Poppy? So late?"

I nodded. "Sorry, Mrs. Carter. I—I—"

"We haven't seen you in a while."

I blinked. *Didn't Keith tell her we broke up?*

"I . . . I know." I peered behind her. The entry hall was dark. "I'm sorry. I hope I didn't wake you. I—"

"No, I was up. Watching a movie. For some reason, ever since we moved to Fear Street, it takes me hours to get to sleep."

"I'm sorry," I said. Awkward. She always had a million complaints. Keith said she was a total hypochondriac. It drove him crazy because there wasn't really anything wrong with her.

"I hope I didn't wake you," I repeated. "But I really need to talk to Keith."

She eyed me suspiciously.

"It's kind of an emergency," I said.

She backed away from the door so I could enter. The house was very warm and smelled of roasted chicken. "He's asleep," she said, studying me. "But I can wake him. Wait here."

"Thank you."

I closed the front door behind me. I stood in the entryway, trying to organize my thoughts. Trying to keep all the fear and suspicion and doubts and anger from swirling around me, capturing me, holding me in this trembling cloud of total confusion.

What am I going to say to Keith? I can't just say, Did you attack Ivy and Jeremy? *But what* can *I say?*

I listened to Mrs. Carter's echoing footsteps going down the long hall to the bedrooms. I shifted my weight. Crossed and uncrossed my arms. Toyed with my bouncy curls for a bit.

Waiting . . . waiting . . .

It was taking a long time. Was she having trouble waking him up?

Was she keeping him in his bedroom until he explained to her why I was here? That would be like her.

Waiting . . .

And then the scrape of her slippers on the hard floor. And she reappeared in the entryway, her long housedress sweeping around her, her face knotted in confusion.

"I . . . I don't understand it," she stammered. She squinted hard at me. "Keith isn't in his room. He's gone."

43

POPPY NARRATES

She shook her head. A lock of blond hair came loose from her ponytail. She raised a hand and struggled to put it back in. "I don't understand it."

"You thought he was home?"

She nodded. "We had dinner. I actually cooked tonight. And then he said he was going out. But . . . I thought he came back. I thought I heard him."

She motioned with one hand. "Come sit down. Tell me what's going on."

I wanted to leave. But she was staring at me with such intensity. And I could see she was mystified about Keith. And a little scared. So I followed her into the family room.

We sat down on brown leather armchairs facing each other. "Do you have any idea where Keith might be?" she asked. She suddenly sounded like a helpless little girl. Like she didn't know how to deal with this at all.

I shook my head. "No. No clue."

"Well, why did you come to see him, Poppy?"

I let out a long sigh. "Do you know about Jeremy and Ivy?" I asked.

She thought for a moment. "No. No, I don't. Have I met them?"

"Probably," I said. "They're good friends. Keith didn't tell you—"

"He doesn't really confide in me," she interrupted. "Keith is very private. He doesn't share much. And ever since we moved here, he's been even more secretive."

"Well, it's not a nice story," I said. "Ivy was attacked in her home. Someone put acid in her shampoo. She has serious burns all over her head."

Mrs. Carter leaned forward, her mouth open in shock. "I can't believe anyone would do that."

"Jeremy had severe allergies." I forced myself to finish the story. "Someone filled his room with hornets, and he was stung to death."

She gasped. "Your friend? He died?"

I nodded. "It's horrible. Horrible."

I could see she was thinking hard. "You don't think Keith had anything to do with any of that, do you, Poppy?"

I took a breath. "Keith was very messed up when I broke up with him. I—"

"You two broke up? I didn't know."

"Well . . . we did. And he acted very weird about it. And . . . and . . . This is very hard, Mrs. Carter. I mean, I don't want to think Keith has attacked my friends. But I just wanted to ask him."

I swallowed hard and raised my eyes to her. "Keith couldn't be responsible—*could* he?"

She stood up and clasped her hands in front of her, pushed them together as if she was praying. Her answer to my question surprised me: "Keith has had episodes before. But I know he's been taking his meds."

I couldn't keep the shock from my face. *Episodes? Meds?*

Keith was definitely a private person. I realized he didn't share anything with his mother, and he hadn't shared anything with me.

"He's not a killer," Mrs. Carter added, crossing her arms tightly in front of her. "No. Keith . . . Keith is afraid of the world. If you broke up with him, it probably was very difficult for him to accept. Rejection has always been hard for him. But . . . but he's not a killer. I know it can't be Keith."

I stood up, and to my surprise, she wrapped me in a hug. She pressed her cheek against mine, and I could feel her body trembling.

"I'm worried," she said softly when she finally let go of me. "I'm very worried, Poppy. Where can Keith be?"

A gentle rain came on as I drove home. The raindrops ran down my windshield, lighted by oncoming cars, and they looked like jewels, a sliding curtain of jewels. The raindrops almost hypnotized me. I guess I wasn't in my right mind.

I don't think I even realized I was driving. I just stared at the flashing raindrops sliding down the glass, lighting up with each passing car.

It was too much for me, too much for my brain to handle. Ivy burned with acid . . . Jeremy murdered . . . Keith disappeared.

Keith . . . I'd spent so much time with him. But there was so much I didn't know. Could Keith be dangerous? Was he paying me back for breaking up with him? I couldn't answer these questions, and I was too frightened and confused to even think about them clearly.

Somehow I made it home. Pulled into the drive, glad to see that Lucas's car was gone. Maybe the police came and chased him away. Maybe they arrested him. I didn't care about Lucas. He was just a creep. I didn't want to let him into my thoughts.

The house was dark and quiet, so quiet I could hear the hum of the refrigerator in the kitchen. I tiptoed to my room. *No way* I wanted to wake Mom or Heather and be bombarded by a hundred questions.

It was after midnight, but I was too wired to feel tired. *Will I ever sleep again?* The faces of my friends flashed before my eyes. Ivy . . . Jeremy . . . Keith . . . They wouldn't go away. They were haunting me. One face after another. And then Jack's face lingered, his arrogant smile, his penetrating eyes . . . Jack.

He was trouble from the start. It was Jack who got us doing the stupid pranks we pulled. Was it possible that he was the one who had turned deadly?

"I have to get some sleep," I said out loud, interrupting my tumbling thoughts.

I changed into my long nightshirt. Brushed my teeth. Looked at my disheveled hair in the bathroom mirror but didn't do anything about it.

Back in my room, I made my way to my bed, still trying to force the faces from my mind. I reached down with both hands, pulled back the covers—and started to scream.

44

POPPY CONTINUES

My scream cut off with a gagging sound and I started to choke. I staggered back from my bed, back from the ghastly, horrifying scene I had uncovered.

Mr. Benjamin, my pet bunny, cut to pieces. His body shredded, his blood spread over my sheet, a dark red puddle. My poor bunny . . . poor Mr. Benjamin . . . murdered.

How? Who?

I couldn't hold it in. I screamed again. Mom and Heather burst into my room. I pointed wildly, my mouth open but unable to speak. I forced down the sour taste of vomit in my mouth.

I watched them approach the bed. Mom uttered a

quiet gasp and covered her face with her hands. Heather screamed and spun away, unable to stand the horror she saw.

The three of us backed away from my bed. Mom shook her head, as if she couldn't believe what she saw. Heather's chest was heaving up and down. She was wheezing with each shallow breath. "No," she muttered. "No. No way."

We huddled out in the hall. An awkward three-way hug didn't last very long. Mom's eyes grew wide. "This means someone was in our house," she said, her voice trembling. "Someone came into our house and did this."

Heather hugged herself tightly. "I . . . I thought I heard footsteps. In the hall. But I thought I was dreaming it."

Mom grabbed Heather's arm. "You *heard* someone?"

Heather nodded. "But I didn't really wake up. I was half asleep . . . dreaming."

I started to sob. "Poor Mr. Benjamin. Who would do that?"

I saw that Heather was crying, too.

"We have to call the police," Mom said. "Someone very dangerous is out to harm everyone. Someone cruel and sadistic . . . and crazy."

Keith, where were you tonight? I wondered. I started back to my room.

Mom grabbed my arm. "Don't touch anything," she said. "The police won't want you to touch anything."

"I just want to change," I said. "I don't want to be in a nightshirt when they get here."

"Just be careful. Don't touch a thing."

I wiped tears off my cheeks as I stepped into my room. I tried to avoid looking at the bed. Just being in the room gave me cold shudders.

Who was in here? Who hated me enough to kill my pet rabbit? Who hated all of us?

I reached for the top dresser drawer to pull out a T-shirt. And something caught my eye. A folded-up sheet of yellow paper on the dresser top. I gazed at it. I didn't remember putting a sheet of paper there.

I grabbed it. Unfolded it. And read the words printed neatly in red ink:

The Shadyside Shade strikes again.

PART FOUR

45

POPPY NARRATES

The next morning, I joined Mom and Heather at the breakfast table, but I couldn't eat. I'd tried to sleep on the couch in the den, but the cushion had buttons on it that hurt my back.

I couldn't sleep anyway. I kept rolling from my side to my back, but the horrifying picture of my murdered rabbit stayed in my mind no matter how I turned.

"I don't want to go to school," I said, cupping my face in my hands.

"You have to go," Mom said, buttering a burned piece of toast. "You didn't go yesterday."

"I can see everyone staring at me," I said. "Everyone watching me . . . afraid of me . . . accusing me. They all think I'm a killer, Mom. They all think—"

"They don't know that you're a victim, too," Mom said. "They don't know what happened here last night."

"It doesn't matter," I said. I picked up the cereal spoon and tapped it tensely on the tabletop. Heather kept sipping her coffee, watching me, not entering the conversation.

"After the fake robbery, I went berserk," I said. "I threatened my friends. I said I'd pay them all back, but I didn't really mean it. I'd never hurt anyone. You know that. But everyone thinks I'm doing these things to get revenge." My voice cracked. "Everyone thinks I'm a murderer. Everyone thinks I killed Jeremy." I tossed the spoon onto the table. "I can't go, Mom. It's just too horrible. No one will talk to me. No one will even come close to me. They'll just stare."

"You have to go," Mom said softly. "You can't let this defeat you. You have to show everyone at school that you're not guilty. If you stay home, they'll just suspect it's because you *are* guilty and you can't face them. You have to stand up to them, Poppy."

I was gripped with fear. Every muscle in my body was clenched. My throat was so tight, I started to choke. "Listen to me," I said, when I could finally speak. "The real killer is at school. I know it. The person who killed Mr. Benjamin last night is there. And that person is dangerous, Mom. Dangerous and crazy."

"The police will find him," Mom said. "Or her."

"You can't be a detective," Heather chimed in. "You can't solve it or find the one who's doing these things. You can't be responsible for that. You just can't."

"I know," I muttered. "I was just saying . . ."

"Go to school and see how it goes," Mom said. "If it's unbearable, you can always come home."

I sighed. "What's happening *is* unbearable," I said. "It's all unbearable. And frightening. And crazy."

"I'll hang out with you at lunch," Heather offered. "That way you won't be alone. It won't be awkward."

I patted her hand. "Sounds like a plan," I said.

Mrs. Gonzalez, the Shadyside High principal, was waiting for me at the front doors. She led me past a group of cheerleaders, who grew quiet as I passed by. "Come sit down." She motioned me into her office and closed the door behind us.

Is she going to suspend me from school?

That isn't fair. I haven't done anything.

I sat down on the edge of the chair facing her desk.

Her desk was cluttered with files and papers. A framed photo of a yellow Lab sat on the corner. She stood behind her chair and studied me.

Mrs. Gonzalez is a tall, middle-aged woman, straight black hair mixed with streaks of gray, pulled back into a single braid. She has big black eyes and wears a lot of mascara to bring them out. Always comes to school in designer suits and stylish skirts and tops. The teachers at Shadyside wear jeans, but she would never be seen in them.

Her expression is often stern, not unfriendly, just kind of businesslike, but no one has anything really bad to say about her, and the teachers seem to like her.

"I like that scarf you're wearing," she started. "You always wear scarves, don't you?"

I nodded. "It's kind of my thing."

"Someone once gave me an Hermès scarf, and I treasured it. That color is beautiful. Perfect with your blond hair."

"Thank you."

She doesn't really want to talk about scarves.

"Poppy, this must be a hard time for you," she said, gripping the back of the chair. "I heard the whole story. I've talked to Ivy. She's back today, by the way."

"Oh. Good," I said awkwardly.

"We have a grief counselor here today for anyone who feels they want to talk about Jeremy." She waited for me to reply, but I couldn't think of anything to say.

The silence grew awkward.

I lowered my head. "I'll really miss him," I whispered.

She nodded. "A roomful of stinging hornets. It must have been horrifying." She sighed. "I can't imagine."

She turned the chair and sat down. She folded her hands on her desk and stared at me with those dark eyes. "Poppy, this is hard to talk about. But you *do* know there are students here, even friends of yours, who think you were responsible."

"I know," I said. "But I didn't—"

"I wanted to give you a chance to talk to me. I thought you might want someone outside your family to confide in." She fumbled with some papers. "I don't know you very well. I guess I know you best from the plays you've been in and the Drama Club. But I'm here if there's anything you want to say or anything I can help you with."

Does she expect me to confess?

Am I supposed to say yes, I'm the one? I'm the killer?

Thank you for letting me get this out in the open. Thank you.

"Thank you," I said, keeping my eyes down. "I'm just so sad . . . so devastated. Ivy and Jeremy were my best friends. And now . . ."

She cleared her throat. "Why do you think people suspect you?"

"Because I threatened them," I blurted out. "Because I said I'd get revenge against them." I pounded my fists on the chair arms. I was losing it and I didn't want to. I didn't want to give anything away to this woman. She wasn't my friend. She wasn't really here to help me.

"But I was just angry," I said. "You say things when you're angry, right? You say things you don't mean."

She nodded. "That's very true. We all do that."

"Well, that's what I did. And now everyone thinks I'm a murderer. Meanwhile, the *real* murderer is walking around, laughing because everyone is blaming me."

That seemed to get to her. Her eyes went really wide and her mouth dropped open. It was as if she had never thought of that. Never thought that the murderer was probably in school today.

She clasped her hands together on the desktop again. "Poppy," she said, her voice hushed, "do you think the murderer is here? Do you think you know who it is?"

I shook my head. "I wish."

"I had a long talk with the police officer who has been assigned the case," she said. "He seemed smart. I know the police will figure it out."

I raised my eyes to her. "I hope so."

"In the meantime, Poppy, it might be hard for you in school. If you want to take a few days off to stay home—"

"I don't think so," I interrupted. "I want to stay in school. I didn't do anything wrong."

She's going to suspend me.

She's going to force me to leave school.

"Okay," she said, nodding. "If anyone gives you a hard time, if anyone assaults you or shouts at you or makes you feel uncomfortable, let me know. Let me know and I'll take care of it immediately. Okay?"

"Uh . . . okay."

I wasn't expecting that. I had a sudden rush of feeling for Mrs. Gonzalez. I wanted to hug her. She was on my side. I thanked her again and walked out of her office.

I started down the hall to my locker. People were hurrying. The first bell was about to ring. I turned the corner and saw Ivy. She was across the hall, just a few feet from me. She wore a big floppy blue wool hat to cover her head.

She saw me, but she pretended she didn't. She spun

completely around and strode off in the other direction.

I sighed. I knew I would never win Ivy over. I had to check her off my list of friends forever.

After all, she had every reason to believe that I was the one who'd nearly burned her head off. I was the last person to visit her that night, the last guest in her house. And I used her bathroom. I was in the bathroom with the shampoo bottle.

She *had* to believe it was me. Who *wouldn't* believe it was me?

I took a deep breath and started walking again. "I can do this," I told myself. "I can make it through the day."

I turned the corner and nearly bumped into Keith.

"Huh?" I gasped. "Keith? You're here?"

46

POPPY CONTINUES

He took a step back. He shifted his backpack on his shoulders. "Of course I'm here. Where else would I be?"

"Well . . . I was at your house last night. Late. You weren't there."

He narrowed his eyes at me. "You were at my house?"

"Your mom didn't know where you were. You weren't in your room and—"

"I stayed at a friend's," he said. "I left her a note on the fridge. But I guess she didn't see it. She never sees my notes. I don't know what I'm supposed to do."

He didn't seem like Keith. He seemed super tense, as if he was lying. Or maybe he just didn't want to talk to me. He kept gazing down the hall, checking to see if anyone was watching us.

"You stayed at a friend's?" I said.

"Yes. Believe it or not, Poppy, I have friends."

He couldn't hide his bitterness, his anger.

"Who did you stay with?"

"It's none of your business, but it was Lucas."

I gasped. "The creepy guy from Harlow's?"

"He isn't creepy when you get to know him. He's a pretty good guy. Weird but good. We've become friends." Keith snickered. "He sure has a crush on you."

"Tell me about it!" I exclaimed. "He attacked me in the parking garage. Seriously. I . . . I can't believe you two are friends."

Keith sneered, an expression I'd never seen on his face before. "I don't care *what* you believe."

The bell rang right above our heads. We both flinched. He shifted his backpack again and walked away.

I watched him till he was at our homeroom at the end of the hall. I thought about him and Lucas. How strange was that? I just couldn't imagine what they had in common. Lucas, the dropout, pushing a broom in a convenience store. Keith, planning to go into premed at Tufts.

Did it make sense in any way?

I made it through the morning without anything terrible happening. I was on super-alert, and my skin kept tingling because kids were looking at me, accusing me. It may have been in my own mind. No one said anything to me. No one tried to confront me, which was a relief.

I had lunch with my sister at a back table in the lunch room. She wanted to talk about her taking acting lessons at the drama school in the Old Village this summer. I just mumbled and tried not to say anything that would start a fight.

What I wanted to say was, *Heather, choose something else. You're not very good-looking and you don't have any talent.* I'm not a cruel person. Sometimes I have cruel thoughts like that, but I had learned my lesson before. I learned I should never try to be honest with my sister. There was just no point to it, and it only resulted in hurt feelings.

After lunch, I saw Jack and Rose tucked away in a corner back by the music room, their arms wrapped around each other, kissing as if their faces were glued together. Jack was facing me, but I don't think he saw me. I think his eyes were closed.

How romantic.

Seeing him there with her sent a shiver down my whole body. I had a million questions I wanted to ask him, mainly about Ivy and Jeremy. I'd always thought Jack was dangerous. But *how* dangerous?

I reminded myself it wasn't my business. I was through with Jack and with Rose. I knew the police must have questioned him. I knew the police must have asked all the questions I wanted to ask.

I had to stop suspecting everyone I saw.

After school, I ran into Manny in the student parking lot. He usually greeted me with a grin, but today his face remained solemn. "How's it going, Poppy?"

I shrugged. "Weird times," I murmured.

He nodded. He stared at me as if he was studying me. I pulled open my car door. "Want a ride home?"

He shook his head. "No. I've . . . uh . . . got to be someplace."

Why is Manny acting so nervous?

Does he think I attacked Ivy and Jeremy?

He hadn't tried to reach me since they were attacked. He hadn't called or texted. It wasn't like him.

He ran a hand back through his straight black hair. "Are you coming to the play tomorrow?"

Since Mr. G's play, starring Rose Groban, had been postponed because of our little car-accident prank, they were performing it in the auditorium in school tomorrow.

I rolled my eyes. "Do I have a choice? It's at one o'clock. Right after lunch. Everyone has to come."

He nodded. "I just thought . . ."

"What? That since I hate Rose, I'd stay home or something? Things are too serious for that kind of stupid jealousy," I said. "Things got too real, Manny."

He nodded. "Too real," he repeated. He waved to a guy at the other end of the parking lot. Then he turned back to me, his usually grinning face still serious. "Are the police still questioning you? Have my brother and his partner—?"

"No. I haven't seen them today," I said. I grabbed his arm. "Why? What did you hear? Did Benny say something to you?"

"No. Not really. I've got to go, Poppy. Catch you later." He took off.

Not really? What did that mean? Why did he say *not really?*

Did Manny think I was the attacker? Did the police still think it was me?

I slammed the car door and sat behind the wheel, staring at the brick wall outside the windshield, just stared at it until it became a rust-colored blur.

How can I make people stop suspecting me?

The horror of the next afternoon didn't help.

47

POPPY NARRATES

After lunch the next afternoon, we were all herded into the auditorium to watch the play. I wanted to sit near the back, out of sight from Rose or anyone else on stage. But I got caught in the stampede and ended up in the third row.

When some kids in the row saw me sit down, they jumped up and moved to the side. Not too subtle. I guessed they didn't want to sit next to a killer. I don't know what they thought I might do, sitting there with my hands in my lap. But they felt they had to move away, to show me how they felt about me.

I yawned. I slid down low in my seat. *Maybe I'll take a nap.*

It was noisy. Everyone was talking and laughing and kidding around. They were all happy about getting out of class for the afternoon to watch a play.

Mrs. Gonzalez came walking down the center aisle. She didn't stop to talk to anyone. But I saw her eyes stop on me for a long moment.

I turned and saw Jack come hurrying down the steps from the stage on the far right. He hopped down the last two steps and disappeared out the auditorium door. I guessed he'd been backstage wishing Rose good luck. Or rather, to break a leg.

Andru Something-or-Other, a foreign-exchange student, sat next to me. He was very big and wide and his body kept pressing against mine, like he was overflowing his seat. I kept edging to the left, but the big guy couldn't help but slide against me.

He was kind of good-looking, with piercing blue eyes that looked like marbles, short sandy hair, and a friendly, toothy smile. But he wore socks under his sandals and didn't have a clue about how to dress. And he didn't speak much English.

I glanced at my phone. One fifteen. Why wasn't the play starting?

Mrs. Gonzalez strode to the center of the stage, a mic

raised in one hand. She started to say something, but Mr. G came trotting over to her from the other side of the stage.

He muttered something in her ear. Then he took the mic from her. "A short delay," he said. He pulled the mic away. It was set too loud. "We are trying to find our star. Please talk among yourselves. It should only be a moment."

Trying to find Rose?

Wouldn't Rose be pumped and ready to finally share her great talent with everyone?

Mr. G said something else to Mrs. Gonzalez, then handed the mic back to her. They both walked off in different directions.

Everyone started talking at once. I kept thinking about what Mr. G had said. *We are trying to find our star.* How weird. Jack must have seen her when he was backstage a few minutes ago.

Andru Something-or-Other bumped me and said something I didn't understand. I asked him to repeat it, and it sounded something like, "Is there a problem?"

I smiled and shrugged. "I don't know. I think it will be okay."

He nodded and adjusted his big body in the seat.

Time passed. I don't know how much. Maybe ten or fifteen minutes. Kids started to clap, encouraging the play to start. And then, finally, the auditorium lights dimmed.

I sat up as I saw the stage curtain start to move. Our curtain doesn't slide from side to side. It goes up and down.

A bright yellow spotlight spread over the maroon curtain as it started to go up. It rose about six or eight feet—and then it stopped.

Some kids gasped when they saw there was something hanging from the curtain, weighing it down, keeping it from rising. It appeared to be a large knot of ropes.

The yellow spotlight concentrated on the large knot. From my seat, it looked like an enormous beehive. But it took only seconds to see that someone was tangled in the ropes.

Someone was in the ropes. Not moving. Arms spread straight out. Eyes wide.

The screams began as everyone recognized Rose Groban.

Rose, strangled in the ropes, her head at such an ugly angle, her hair falling down the side of her lifeless head.

I screamed, too. I screamed at the most horrifying

scene I had ever witnessed. Screamed in terror and fright, even though it was Rose. Beautiful Rose. Dead in the curtain. Strangled to death.

And, *oh no!*

Oh no! Oh no!

Was that *my* scarf around her neck?

48

POPPY CONTINUES THE STORY

The police took over the music room and set it up as their headquarters to question people. No one was allowed to go home.

The halls were filled with kids sobbing and hugging each other and wandering the halls in distress, despite teachers' efforts to herd them back to their classrooms.

I've never seen so many people in shock before, and it was distressing and frightening, and I knew I'd have nightmares about Rose strangled in my scarf in the stage ropes for the rest of my life.

Of course, I was the first one called in to be questioned. I entered the room to find Officer Raap seated at a table, and another cop I'd never seen before standing beside him. Benny Kline was not in the room.

"This is Lieutenant Marshall," Raap said, his eyes studying me as I came closer.

Marshall reached out to shake hands. He was big, broad-shouldered, African American, with close-shaved hair, and a silver ring in one ear. He didn't wear a uniform. He wore a stylish gray suit that fit him perfectly.

His hand was twice as big as mine, but he had a gentle handshake, and his expression was sympathetic, as if he realized how terrible it was for me to have to be questioned about this horrifying murder.

They motioned for me to sit down. Then Marshall sat down across from me. "Officer Raap has been telling me about you, Poppy." He had a surprisingly light voice, almost a whisper.

I lowered my head. "Did he say anything good?"

"He brought me up to date on what happened to some of your friends." He patted the back of my hand. "This has to be a hard time for you," he said, locking his brown eyes on mine.

I nodded. "It's been . . . horrible."

"Poppy, how did your scarf get around Rose Groban's neck?" Raap chimed in, all business. "Do you have an explanation for us?"

I swallowed. "Not really. I mean, I don't know how it got there. I don't—"

"Did you give it to her?" Raap asked. "Did you go onstage at all today?"

"No. No way," I said, feeling the emotion rise in my chest. "Look. I'm totally shocked that scarf was anywhere near her. I mean, more than shocked. I don't understand it. I really don't." My voice cracked.

I took a deep breath—and then I remembered something. "Lucas," I said. "This guy Lucas. He attacked me in the taxi garage. He—he took my scarf."

"Hold on a second," Marshall said, raising a hand as if to say *halt*. "You say you were attacked?"

I nodded.

"Did you report it?"

"No," I said softly. "I . . . I didn't want more trouble. I just . . . wanted to forget about it. But Lucas pulled off the scarf that I was wearing, and he took it away from me."

"We'll talk to Lucas," Raap said to Marshall. He turned back to me. "Is he in school today? Have you seen him?"

"No," I answered. "He doesn't go here. He dropped out."

Raap narrowed his eyes at me. "He doesn't go to school here? Then how did he wrap your scarf around Rose's neck this afternoon?"

I shrugged. "I don't know. I just can't imagine." Then I had a thought. "Lucas has a friend here. Keith Carter. Maybe Lucas gave the scarf to Keith."

"But why would Keith Carter murder Rose Groban?" Marshall demanded.

"Keith has been totally weird lately. I broke up with him a couple of weeks ago. And he didn't take it well. He was angry. Well . . . beyond angry."

Both cops stared hard at me. I could see suspicion on Raap's pale face. I couldn't read Marshall at all. A hush fell over the room. I could hear someone crying out in the hall.

"You think Lucas gave the scarf to Keith?" Marshall said finally. He slid an iPad onto the table and typed some words. "And Keith murdered Rose? Why? Why would he do that?"

I let out a sob. "Someone has been attacking my friends one by one. Two people I know were murdered. Jeremy and Rose."

Raap scratched his mop of red hair. "And you think Keith might be crazy enough—"

"I don't like ratting out my friends!" I exclaimed, suddenly losing it. "Maybe I'm totally wrong. Maybe I'm crazy. But I'm trying to help you. I'm trying to help you make it *stop*."

Raap ignored my emotional plea. He turned to Marshall. "Call Randy at the station. Let's get someone to talk to this guy Lucas." He turned back to me. "Where did you say we could find him?"

"I didn't. He works at Harlow's. You know. The convenience store on River Road. He's, like, a janitor there."

Marshall crossed the room, his phone to his ear. I heard him telling someone at the station to bring Lucas in. Raap continued to stare at me, his expression thoughtful, like he was trying to figure out what to ask me next.

"Can I go now?" I asked finally.

"Do you have anything else to tell us?"

"No," I said. "But if I think of something . . ."

"Go to your homeroom and wait," Raap said, motioning to the door with one hand. "No one goes home till we figure this out." He pulled himself up straight. "We're going to solve this today. I promise you that. This will all stop today."

I climbed to my feet. I didn't know what to say to that.

"We'll talk to Keith next," Raap said. "See what his story is."

I was nearly to the door when Marshall called me back. He lowered his phone from his ear. He turned to Raap. "This Lucas has an alibi," he said. "He's been at Harlow's since seven this morning. Harlow backs him up."

Raap's eyes were on me. "You can cross him off your list, Poppy."

I nodded and headed out the door. I just wanted to get out of that room, away from their questions and their accusing eyes.

Some distraught-looking kids were huddled in groups in the hall, talking quietly, shaking their heads. Teachers were trying to round them up and get them into class-rooms until they were allowed to leave the building.

I passed the auditorium on my way to my homeroom. The doors were open, and I could see that police officers crawled over the entire stage. They all wore blue latex gloves and blue things that looked like shower caps over their shoes.

Crime shows on TV are very entertaining. A few years ago, Ivy and I were addicted to some true-crime shows. We loved the phony reenactments.

But when you see a murder being investigated by real cops in a real murder scene, it's a whole different feeling. It just makes you want to vomit.

I stopped and watched the cops working on the stage. The spotlight was still shining a circle of yellow light on the play backdrop. No one had turned it off.

I just couldn't get the picture out of my mind of Rose with her eyes bulging, her body tangled in the ropes, and my scarf wrapped so tightly around her neck.

A figure came striding toward me. Mr. G, his eyes straight forward, his expression grim, hands shoved deep in his pants pockets.

"Hey, Mr. G. I—" I started.

But he walked right past me without slowing. "Can't talk," he murmured. He didn't look back.

I turned the corner and stepped into my homeroom. Some kids were milling up at the front of the room. I took a seat in the back. I clasped my hands together and shut my eyes.

This is the longest, most horrible day of my life.

After a few minutes, I felt someone tap my shoulder from behind. I turned to see Miss Kellogg, the home-room teacher. "Poppy, are you okay?"

"Not really," I said.

"Is there anything I can do?"

"Can you back up time a day?"

She shook her head. "I don't think so. There are sodas for everyone in the lunchroom, if you'd like. I don't know how long they're going to keep everyone here."

"Thanks," I murmured. I kept my eyes closed tight, but it didn't help shut out the horrifying picture of Rose strangled in the curtain.

As it turned out, the wait in homeroom wasn't long. Miss Kellogg told me the police wanted to see me back in the music room. I made the long walk, feeling weary—weary and afraid. The auditorium was still crawling with cops.

I stepped into the music room to find that several kids were already there. Ivy sat at the long table next to Lieutenant Marshall. Her big floppy hat had fallen to one side, revealing the bandage underneath.

Jack sat across from her. His eyes kept darting from side to side, revealing his nervousness. He glanced at me for a moment, then quickly turned away.

Manny sat two chairs down from Ivy. He sprawled on the chair, put both shoes up on the table, acting casual.

Keith stood against the wall, hands in his jeans pockets. He nodded at me as I came into the room.

I heard footsteps behind me and turned, surprised to see my sister entering the room. "Heather? You're here?" I blurted out.

She shrugged. I couldn't read her expression. Her top was too small for her. It made her stomach look like she had a watermelon under her blouse.

I scolded myself for thinking that. But you can't control your thoughts, especially in tense, frightening situations.

Raap was watching me. I could tell he wanted me to take the seat next to him. But I stepped next to Keith and leaned against the wall beside him.

Heather plopped down in a chair at the far end of the table. She fiddled with her hair but seemed perfectly calm.

Keith was sweating and his face was pink. Standing next to him, I could feel the heat coming off his body. I guessed that the two cops had questioned him pretty hard.

I knew that Keith didn't like a lot of questions thrown at him. He panicked at tests, too, and sometimes had to take them over again.

He was gazing straight ahead, breathing a little hard. It gave me a chance to study him. What had he told them?

Did he know anything about Rose's death? Jeremy? Ivy's acid attack?

"I think we have the whole group together," Raap said, his eyes still on me. "Have we left anyone out?"

No one answered.

"We are determined to solve this right away," he continued. "We have been gathering DNA evidence on the stage. Lieutenant Marshall and I have talked to you all. And we have—"

"But have any of you thought of anything else that could be helpful?" Marshall interrupted. "Anything at all? Something you heard. Something you saw. A rumor. Gossip of any kind."

"Poppy was the last one to visit me at my house," Ivy said. She didn't turn around. She kept her back to me. "No one else could have put the acid in my shampoo bottle."

"We talked about this," Raap said, sounding impatient. "We already said what if someone sneaked into your house and you didn't know it, Ivy."

A picture flashed into my mind. "Oh, wow," I murmured.

"Poppy, what is it?" Marshall asked.

"Oh, wow. I just thought of something." I glanced at

Jack. He was tapping his fingers on the table. He didn't look at me but kept his gaze on the table.

"Tell us," Marshall urged.

I hesitated. It was hard to talk about someone when they were right in the room with you. And . . . how dangerous was Jack? Would he attack me if I told what I'd seen?

"Come on, Poppy," Raap said, motioning for me to hurry up. "What is it? What were you going to tell us?"

I kept my eyes on Jack. His lips tightened and he glared at me, warning me. But I didn't care. It was too late to be scared. Too many people were dead or ruined.

"I saw Jack running from the stage," I said. "Just before the curtain was pulled. He must have been backstage. And I saw him run down the stairs and out the side door of the auditorium."

I got all that out in a single breath. And I watched Jack the whole time I was talking. Watched his face grow tighter and his eyes grow wider. Watched him clench his hands into fists on the tabletop.

I could feel the tension in the room rise. Keith shifted his weight, edged away from me. The two cops turned to Jack. Marshall's fingers were squeezing the table edge.

All eyes were on Jack because of my accusation.

"What's the story?" Raap asked him.

Jack cleared his throat. His face was tomato red now. "I . . . was looking for Rose. That's all. I wanted to tell her to break a leg. I knew it was time for the play to start. But I just wanted to wish her good luck. You know."

"And did you wish her good luck?" Marshall asked.

Jack scowled at him. "Obviously not. I couldn't find her. She wasn't with the other actors in the wings. And she wasn't in the dressing room."

He brushed back his hair with a swift motion. His eyes were still wide, as if frightened. "I didn't find her. So I left the stage and walked out of the auditorium. That's all. I didn't *run* out, like Poppy just said. I walked down the steps and out the door." He stared at the officers, as if defying them. "That's all. Really. No more to the story."

"We're wasting our time," Ivy suddenly chimed in. She turned and glanced at me, then quickly turned back to the two cops. "We all know Poppy killed Rose," she said. "We all know that Poppy hated—"

"Stop!" I screamed. "What are you *saying*? Are you *crazy*?" I took a few steps toward Ivy.

Marshall jumped to his feet, his arms stretched out at his sides, ready to stop me if he needed to. "Stop right there, Poppy. Let her finish."

I stood there, off balance, ready to pounce, breathing hard.

"Did Poppy tell you how much she hates Rose?" Ivy said to the cops. "Did Poppy tell you she swore she'd get revenge on all of us? Did she tell you that?"

Ivy swung around in her chair. Her eyes were wild and her face was tight with anger. The hat slid off her head, and I could see the deep black burn marks poking out from the edge of her bandage.

"Why don't you just confess, Poppy?" she screamed. "Everyone knows it was you. Why don't you just tell the truth and end all this?"

I took a deep breath. "Okay," I said breathlessly, my heart pounding, my chest heaving up and down. "Okay. I confess. I did it all."

49

POPPY CONTINUES

The room filled with shocked gasps. Ivy nearly fell off her chair. The two cops eyed me with new concentration.

"Would you repeat that?" Raap said quietly.

"Are you confessing to these murders?" his partner demanded.

I nodded. "Yes. I confess." I let out a sob. "Everyone knows it anyway. I might as well come clean. It will only be a matter of time." I lowered my head. My shoulders began to tremble.

Marshall jumped to his feet. His body was tense, his arms out from his sides, as if expecting a fight, or expecting me to run. "Poppy, don't say another word," he ordered. "I'm going to read you your rights. Officer

Raap and I are arresting you for the murders of Jeremy Klavan and Rose Groban."

I didn't move from where I was standing. I raised my hands to make it easier for him. I kept my head lowered in surrender. I avoided the eyes of the others in the room.

Marshall strode toward me. Raap was on his feet now, his expression solemn, standing a few feet behind his partner.

"Wait! Stop!" A voice rang out.

Heather came stumbling toward the two officers.

They turned, startled. The plastic cuffs rattled in Marshall's hands.

"Stop!" Heather cried. "Poppy is a liar. She's trying to protect me. She—"

"No, I'm not!" I cried.

"Shut up, Poppy. You're a liar," Heather cried. "Don't try to take the blame. I did it. I did it all. Everything!"

"But, Heather—" I said.

"I did it because I *hate* you, Poppy, and I hate your friends," Heather said, her voice hoarse and shrill. She spun around, giving everyone a furious scowl.

"You all treated me like I was invisible. You walked past me and ignored me, and you left me out of everything. I hate you all. I hate you! I *hate* you!"

She swung her fists in a fury above her head. Suddenly,

she stopped and turned to me. "When did you figure out it was me?"

I raised my eyes to her. "It . . . it took me a while," I stammered. "But I realized you knew about the hornets in Mom's lab. And you were the only other one who knew about the acid I used in the basement."

I took a breath. My heart was pounding. "And it was so easy for you to come into my room at any time and take one of my scarves to murder Rose with. And—"

"But, why?" Ivy interrupted. "Heather, why did you kill Rose?"

"Because she had no time for me. She dumped me as soon as she and Jack started making nice to each other. Once Jack was in the picture, I was like a bug she wanted to step on."

Heather took a step toward Ivy. Marshall moved quickly to block her path. She turned back to me.

"That night you threw my trophy into the wall. I knew there was something wrong with you," I told her. "But I had no idea . . ."

Everyone screamed as Heather pulled a knife from her pocket. The long blade gleamed as she raised it above her head. "I'm not finished, Poppy. I'm so sorry . . . So sorry."

She dove forward and plunged the knife deep into my chest.

50

POPPY NARRATES

I uttered a groan of pain, shut my eyes, and slid to my back on the floor. I gripped the knife firmly in both hands as I went down.

Screams. Cries. Startled gasps. The ceiling spun above my head.

Keith's shout rose over the commotion: "Stop this! Stop this! This is crazy! I did it! Not Heather. I did everything."

Keith grabbed Heather from behind and shoved her away. "You didn't want to know me! None of you!" he screamed. "I wasn't good enough for Poppy! I wasn't good enough for any of you. You didn't want to know me. No one wanted to know me. No one—"

Marshall made a grab for him. But, his eyes wild,

his face bright red, Keith backed out of the cop's reach. "I wanted to kill you ALL!" he screeched. "You didn't know me. No one knew me."

He grabbed his shirt with both hands—and ripped it away. The buttons went flying. He swung his shirt off and tossed it onto the floor.

"Oh no!" I cried. My cry was drowned out by the other wails of surprise in the room.

Keith's arms and chest . . . They were covered in red cuts and ugly bruises and scabs. I couldn't see any skin on his shoulders, just deep red cut marks.

"You don't know me! Do you see? *Do* you? You don't know me!" he shrieked.

Marshall wrapped an arm around Keith's shoulders and pulled him away.

Raap dropped down beside me, his face filled with concern. "Poppy, are you—"

I sat up and raised the knife above my chest. I pushed the blade in and let it slide out. "It's the fake knife we use for plays," I explained to the startled, goggle-eyed cop. "See? The blade slides into the handle?"

I handed the knife to my sister. "Heather, you're a better actress than I thought you were."

She grinned and reached both hands down to pull

me to my feet. "We're a good team," she said. "See? We certainly fooled everyone in the room."

I slid my arm around her shoulders. "Everyone believed us."

Raap narrowed his eyes at me. "So you two cooked up that whole act?"

I nodded. "In the hall. Just now. We figured if we confessed, the real culprit wouldn't be able to just stand by."

"Stabbing Poppy with the knife was *my* idea," Heather said.

I shoved her. "I think you enjoyed that too much."

Heather laughed. "Well . . . your dying scene was your best yet. Mr. G would be proud."

Marshall was struggling to get Keith's shirt back on him as he pulled him out of the room. Raap followed, but turned back to the rest of us. "We'll need statements from you all," he said. They disappeared into the hall.

Ivy walked over and wrapped me in a hug. "I'm so sorry, Poppy. So sorry I accused you."

"It's okay," I choked out.

"We all jumped to conclusions," Manny said, mopping sweat off his forehead.

I kept my arm around Heather's shoulder. "Well, I'll

tell you one thing," I said, "I think we're cured. I don't think any of us want to be famous anymore."

Heather's eyes flashed. "'O Romeo, Romeo,'" she burst out. "'Wherefore art thou, Romeo?'"

I wanted to tell her that was terrible. But then I figured, it could wait till later.

Return to R.L. STINE'S terrifying world of FEAR STREET